CLANDESTINE CONFESSIONS

NINA HOLDEN

CLANDESTINE CONFESSIONS

Gavta Publishing

Clandestine Confessions
Published by Gavta Publishing 2005

ISBN 90 9019422 3

D/2005/10555/1

For J.E.M.

Climbing the wet subway stairs that led up to the streets, my ears were drawn to the laughter of two male teenage voices that could be heard above the early morning tumult.

"No, we'll rape her first. Then we'll steal her money," one of the voices added excitedly. They both agreed, laughing.

I felt chilled but continued to place one foot in front of the other until I reached the top of the stairs where I took a few deep breaths and brushed away the tears that had come into my eyes. It was the third time in two days that I had overheard conversations trivializing this crime, a crime that had changed my life forever.

I was raised a Catholic girl and truly believed that I would only sleep with one man and that that man would be my husband. I had dreamed of sharing that special intimacy only with him, and, although I hadn't met this man, I was saving myself for him, and only him. But that was not to be my fate.

Chapter 1

Despite the fact that the Caribbean sun was cruelly hot, I felt as though I were freezing as I made my way across the cobbled streets of St. Catherine's to the doctor's office.

I had decided to have tests done. I was on the pill, although I took it for menstrual cramps, not birth control. Now I was glad. At least I did not have to worry about being pregnant.

A metal plaque on the wooden door reassured me that I was at the right place. I pushed the door open and was hit by the air conditioning that lowered the outside temperature by at least twenty degrees. Finding myself in a brightly lit hallway, I followed the sign that said "WAITING ROOM" around the corner and to the left. I carefully stuck my head in the door to catch a glimpse of the unknown territory. The less anyone saw of me, the easier it would be for me to get away.

The nurse who was standing on the other side of the room must have been able to tell there was something very wrong when I entered, although a brief glance in her direction was all I could manage. I dropped into the hard wooden chair closest to the door. I was in, but I could still get out.

"What's the matter, honey?" the nurse asked. Her voice was concerned.

I didn't budge and heard her high–heeled shoes clicking against the marble floor. Then her soft long fingers were brushing my cheek. Cupping my face in her hand, she raised my chin. It was clear that she would not put up with any nonsense. Yet her chocolate brown eyes were gentle. She was wearing a white nurse's cap.

White. The color that represented purity and innocence was a color I was no longer privileged to wear. My white wedding dress should now be ecru or perhaps blue or pink. No, it could not be pink. That was the color of my vaginal blood that had already been spilt. I was no longer a virgin. The physical evidence was there. There could never be another first man for me again. And the color of my gown would have to be blue, blue to represent the old, what I once was and was now pretending to still be.

What had become of me? How could I have allowed myself to be reduced to this being not worthy of any respect, and that all in a matter of minutes?

I couldn't tell the nurse I had been raped. I couldn't bring myself to say that wretched word, certainly not about myself. But I had to tell her something.

"I've had unprotected sex," I said, carefully watching her eyes for any clues as to what she might be thinking. "And I want to be examined to make sure I didn't catch any diseases," I added hesitantly.

I didn't really want that, of course, but it had to be done. I could only imagine what the nurse must have thought of me. She took in a deep breath and exhaled through her nose. I felt the moist air on my cheek.

"All right, come in here," she said, leading me into an examining room. "Take off your slacks and underwear and lie down here. I'll go get the doctor."

For a brief moment I was left alone in the artificially lit, windowless room. The plaster on the walls and ceiling was cracked. Beside the examination table there were only a stool and a wooden cabinet containing all sorts of medical instruments, bottles of what I assumed to be disinfecting liquids, and cotton. I removed my clothes.

I was still sitting on the end of the examination table with my legs crossed, pulling my T–shirt down as far as it could go, when the doctor came in. He was a dark–haired sturdy–looking man.

I had arrived on the island only two months earlier to work in a hotel. Still being eighteen, I had initially been considered too young, but the interviewer had decided to give me a chance. That had been my big break.

Although I was eighteen, I looked younger, perhaps because I was only five foot five and weighed 105 pounds, a childlike girl with gray–blue eyes and light brown hair. Mainly of Swiss descent — my father's father was from Luxembourg — I had been raised in the States.

The nurse told me to lie down. She then put a towel over my lower body. The doctor, who I guessed to be in his early forties, gave me a firm look, straight into my eyes. Could he see through me? Did he see the label "rape" on my face, or would I still qualify for careless? He sat down and began his examination. And when he did, I started to cry and couldn't stop. It was just too much. And it *did* hurt. Clearly this was not a reaction the nurse and doctor had anticipated.

"I know this is uncomfortable, but it won't be much longer," the nurse said, trying to comfort me. She came around the table to stand beside me, taking my hand and squeezing it. As for the doctor, he stopped the examination and tried to settle me down.

"Shh," he said. "It's okay. I'm just taking a look to make sure everything's all right. There's nothing to worry about. We'll be done in no time."

He gently stroked my leg. I lifted my upper body to check where he was touching me. He continued to rub my leg so I could see the exact place. It was all right. His big brown eyes seemed to be trying to tell me he genuinely cared.

His soothing voice reminded me of a teacher I'd had in kindergarten, a man who had always known precisely how to comfort a child in distress. But it wasn't working now, probably because I wasn't a child anymore. I was a grownup dealing with very grownup issues. Or at least trying to.

I lay down again, nodding at the doctor to indicate that it was all right for him to proceed. He hesitated.

"Please hurry up and get it over and done with," I begged him.

He came to sit beside me on the examination table then.

"Were you sexually abused as a child?" he asked. "Because your behavior isn't normal. Are you sure no one ever abused you when you were a little girl? Perhaps an uncle, a neighbor…"

It was time to come clean. Knowing very well that the spoken words would make the truth real. I sat up. The doctor gently brushed my hair out of my face. His hand felt coarse and sweaty, but his eyes reflected his true nature, his kindness and his generosity. I took a deep breath and spoke the words that would forever categorize me and make me a victim for the rest of my life.

"I was raped," I said in a soft voice, suddenly very aware of the difficulty my lips experienced forming these words, the most painful words I had ever spoken.

My eyes filled with tears at the touch of the doctor's warm hands on my head. I could not bear to be comforted just now.

"I know I have to go through this," I said sobbing, "so let's just get it over and done with before I change my mind."

"When did this happen?" he asked softly.

"Friday evening," I said. "I know I should have come here directly, but he made me shower. There was…there was no evidence left."

I remembered how the rapist had pulled me into the bathroom. He had already raped me. What was he going to do now, drown me? I had stood there crying, bending over, trying to cover my body as much as I could. Still keeping a tight grip on me, he had turned on the water and shoved the showerhead in my hand, although I could barely hold it.

"Rinse yourself," he ordered me.

He was pushing my legs open trying to get his hand inside me. I did it myself. I couldn't have him touch me there anymore. My groin hurt. I had to do it thoroughly as he was watching closely, holding my legs open.

"Please carry on," I said to the doctor, now brushing away my tears.

"Are you sure you're going to be all right?" he asked me.

"It's not as though I have much choice," I said.

Because I was not going to be all right. I knew that the moment I had felt that man enter my body that a big part of me had died. And that is how I felt. Dead. Nothing mattered anymore. I was no longer really present in this world. The body that had once stood gracefully and proud was now a plundered ruin. A phallus had dug its way through my body, like an apple corer, leaving me with an empty hole inside.

The doctor continued the examination, stopping at regular intervals to remind me to keep breathing normally. But it was painful to have anyone touch me there, let alone put anything inside me. Although both the doctor and his nurse tried to comfort me, I could not stop weeping until, finally, he was done.

"I'm going to check this under the microscope," he said. "I'll be right back."

A few minutes later he returned. "All the test results I have so far are negative," he said softly, giving me an encouraging smile and pinching my cheek. "Call me next week, on Monday, after two, about the blood tests. But you have to be tested again after six months to be absolutely sure about HIV. Do you have any family here?" he asked in a fatherly manner.

I shook my head. Even if my family had been here, I knew that I would not have been able to bring myself to tell them what had happened because I was so ashamed. And I was afraid that they would blame me. How could I have been so stupid as to rinse myself? But I'd had no choice. I also worried that if I went home now, my family would think that I wasn't able to take care of myself: I'd only just left.

The doctor kissed his hand and then held it against my cheek.

"Come back if you ever want to talk," he added.

I thanked him. But I never went back.

In spite of my doubts, I decided to be brave and to report what had happened to the authorities. Even though the attacker had not attempted to take my life, I could not let him get away with what he had done because he would surely do it again to someone else. If I did not take charge now, I knew I would never be strong enough to make a report. It was act now or forever hold your peace. And I certainly no longer knew the meaning of peace.

As a consequence, that same morning, I headed for the market square in St. Catherine's, only a few blocks away from the doctor's office. I had bought myself an overpriced coke, as I had felt faint after the medical examination. As much as I dreaded reporting the crime, I couldn't put it off any longer.

Friday night I had lain there, crying on the floor in my apartment for what must have been hours, curled up in a ball, hoping to disappear into the rough carpet beneath me. Saturday I had spent drowning in my own tears, and Sunday I had called in sick. I had to report what had happened to the police now, before I returned for the Monday afternoon shift and tried to pick up my life again as if nothing had happened. After spending an entire weekend alone in my apartment in tears, too ashamed to face the outside world, I had to take charge now, no matter what the outcome might be.

I knew the doctor would take care of any medical issues. But what could the police do now that I had washed away all the evidence?

I felt so alone. I couldn't confide in my colleagues because they were acquainted with the man who had raped me and I was afraid that they wouldn't believe me. On top of that, I had showered. I couldn't prove anything, which is why I had seen no need in going to the doctor straight away. I just felt so incredibly guilty about the humiliating experience I had been through.

Now I crossed the square, passing the statue of St. Catherine, toward the police station, trembling as I entered. This was me, going to report a rape. My rape.

A young female officer neatly clad in her blue uniform came up to me. I was relieved it was a woman.

"What can I do for you?" she asked, looking at me curiously.

"Okay, take a deep breath and speak," I told myself. But I just wanted to turn and run. If I didn't report the assault then maybe it hadn't happened and I could have my life back, no questions asked. But my feet were stuck. They wouldn't move. I couldn't run away. It was too late.

"What can I do for you?" she asked me again.

"I'm here to report a crime," I said, trying to avoid the issue for as long as possible.

"What kind of crime?" the officer asked me.

She showed genuine concern. But I needed more from her than that. Something had to be done.

"I'm here to report a rape," I whispered.

"Yours?" she asked.

That wasn't fair. She couldn't make it mine, like something I owned. I felt as though someone had shoved something into my hands that I didn't want to hold. Like in school, in music class, when you were made to hold the worst possible instrument. You couldn't just put it down next to you, trying to distance yourself from it. You had to hold it, so that everyone would know that it was yours.

Embarrassed, I stared at my shoes until she took my arm and led me down the hall.

I followed her, still staring at the floor. It seemed important somehow that no one see my face. Sometimes on TV you saw people who tried to cover their face when they were being arrested. I knew how they felt now. I did not want my face being associated with this crime. I felt more like a criminal than a victim. Dirty. Guilty. Ashamed.

Once we had reached the right office, the female officer left me alone with two policemen who were working at their desks. The office she had brought me to was small, dark and stuffy, almost all the space taken up by the two wooden desks topped with computers and huge piles of paperwork. I looked at the officers, and they looked back at me. I had no intention of speaking first.

"Why don't you come sit down and tell us what happened?" the tall middle–aged officer suggested.

I walked over to his desk and noticed that the short plump policeman, who I guessed to be in his early twenties, was watching me closely. There was something about the way he was looking at me that gave me the creeps.

Somehow I got my story out, using tissue after tissue to wipe my eyes. If simply reporting this to the police was so difficult, how would I ever hold up if this went to court?

"That's terrible," the tall officer said. "It's awful how some people behave like animals. Something should really be done about it. We hear about these things all the time. You're brave. Most girls don't even report it. And that's how these monsters keep getting away with it."

I was aware of a ray of hope. He was going to pay attention to what had happened to me. He would do something about it.

But instead he and the younger policeman turned their backs toward me and lowered their voices, apparently to discuss my case.

"Now, I've taken note of it," the middle–aged officer said, "and I'll get back to you once I've had the chance to look into this."

"Could you check if he's already in your system?" I asked the officers. "Maybe he's done this to someone else before."

"How well do you know this man?" the elder of the two asked me.

I tried to explain to the policemen that he was someone I'd been briefly introduced to at work and that I had seen him there just that one time, fully realizing that with this information it would be much more difficult to convince them that he had done this to me against my will. I had no bruises to show them. No proof that I had tried to fight him off. He had been too heavy for me to push away. But who would believe that?

The middle–aged officer left the room and soon returned with a file in his hands.

"We looked in our system," he said, "and you're lucky. We found him. The man who attacked you already has a criminal record. In fact, he has been in jail for violence."

"Has he attacked another woman before?" I asked, wondering if violence was his euphemism for rape.

"I'm sorry, we can't give you any specific details on the other case," he said. "It's against our policy."

I suppose that was understandable. But I was lucky. He *was* a criminal. I had been right to come here, despite my doubts. I was so relieved by the news, I could not hold back my tears.

The tall officer handed me another tissue. I knew that he was doing his best to make me feel comfortable.

"We'll get back to you then," the younger officer told me.

But I didn't understand. I had given them a name. I had actually told them where the rapist worked. Basically, I had done a large part of their job for them.

Checking to make sure they had at least taken note of it, I asked, "But you did put it in your system, right?"

"Yes," the elder of the two now replied. "And if he ever does it again, we'll know he's raped someone before."

And it also came to me, for the first time, that just being in another country where customs were different was bound to make everything more difficult.

"When will you get back to me?" I asked, hoping that the time frame would be something I could handle.

"That could be a while," the plump one replied. "We're swamped."

"Do I need a reference number?" I asked, desperate to have something in my hands.

The middle–aged officer now gave me the rapist's file number.

"How long did you say you were here for?" he asked me.

"I'll be leaving the island in May," I said.

"Don't worry," he told me. "You've got plenty of time. Besides, there's no hurry. The term of limitation is three years."

Convinced by now that this was the best response I was going to get, I left. At least I had accomplished something. I had made a formal report, and I had the number of the rapist's file as well as the names of the policemen to whom I had made the report.

I tried to comfort myself with the thought that I still had quite some time before the case expired. The main thing was that I had reported the assault now.

But the officers never got back to me. I was baffled by the lack of official response. I might be in the Caribbean, but this was still a part of the Western world and I would have thought that crimes like rape would be dealt with firmly. No wonder so few victims reported a rape. That made sense now. I tried calling the officers a few times, but I was afraid to press the subject because I did not want police retaliation.

I found that I didn't trust anyone. Perhaps I should just forget all about justice. The doctor hadn't even suggested I report the rape to the police. I wondered why. I felt incredibly alone and lost. And I felt so guilty and ashamed. If the police wouldn't arrest him even after having seen that he had a record of violent behavior, then what could I do?

It all seemed overwhelmingly difficult. I had to rely on public transportation and public phones. I didn't have enough money to hire a lawyer. And since I still had to wait six months to be absolutely certain that I hadn't contracted HIV, I had no choice but to get on with my life and shut out the experience while I waited. I could have just quit my job and gone back home. But then the rapist would have ruined even more of my life. Little did I know that he had already caused much more damage than I ever could have imagined.

***

The company the rapist worked for was on my way to work, and I was terrified that we might encounter one another, although I guessed that by the time I was due for most of my shifts at the hotel, a repairman like him would be out on the job, and when I had to work early mornings or return late at night the building would be closed. There was no use making a detour as I would then have to walk through more deserted areas.

One afternoon about a month after the incident, I had to go inside the office building to get some papers since the hotel I was working at had hired this company to make repairs on staff apartments. In fact, the bellboy had introduced me to the man who would become my rapist, along with some of his colleagues, all of them repairmen. That was the only time I had ever seen any of them at the hotel.

Now, terrified, I entered the modern–looking building and went to the reception.

"I'm here to see Mr. Rossi," I said, worried that my voice would tremble.

"Go up to the sixth floor," the receptionist told me, not even bothering to look up from his book. "The elevators are down the corridor on the left."

I hurried down the corridor as I noticed the elevator was filling up quickly. To my surprise, I still fitted in.

"It's pretty crowded in here," a clearly annoyed woman remarked.

"More room for you now," a man said, getting off when we got to the second floor, along with several others.

When we reached the third floor, everyone got off, except for me and a man at the back. It was he! I had hoped that I would never again see his threatening brown eyes and the dark–colored birthmark on his chin. Grabbing my arm, he pulled me toward the back of the elevator.

I must have briefly lost control of my bladder as I felt my urine trickling down my legs. It was still three more floors to the sixth floor. But just then we came to a stop at the fourth floor and he let go of me when two men in suits entered. One of them pressed the button for the sixth floor. I was extremely relieved.

My hands were trembling, so that it was difficult for me to get my sunglasses out of my bag to cover my teary eyes. The two men and I got out on the sixth floor. He didn't.

I was shivering by the time I entered the pale blue office and asked for Mr. Rossi, who wasn't in. However, his secretary gave me a package, saying that he had left it with her to give to me. I was happy to just take it and get out.

When I returned to the elevator, there was an elderly man waiting.

"Are you going back down to the reception?" I asked him, holding my breath until he answered. I nearly wept when he said he was.

There was no chance that I would be alone with that criminal again.

23

Squeezing my legs together to try to stop the leaking, I hurried out of the building. With tears rolling down my cheeks I ran down the street until I reached a tavern where a young man clad in jeans and a T–shirt pointed me into the direction of the restroom.

I was petrified. If the police had only arrested him like they should have, this would not have happened. The encounter with the rapist had literally made me sick, and, because I was so disgusted by the touch of his hand on my skin, I took some soap and scrubbed my arm until it almost bled.

"I poured you a drink," the tall dark–skinned fellow told me when I came out. "I put it on the bar counter for you. It's free."

He continued to clean the outside tables and chairs with the cloth he had just wet in the bucket beside him. I sat down on one of the wooden bar stools and sipped my coke. The dim, cool room with its beamed ceiling, wooden–topped tables and cane chairs had a calming effect on me.

"Are you all right?" the young man asked as he came back in.

I nodded, but the look in his eyes told me he didn't believe me.

"Do you want something to eat?" he asked me, folding his arms on the counter.

"No, I'm all right," I said. "But thank you."

Whatever I ate I would probably just throw up again anyway. And I had to go back to work.

So I finished the drink, got up and handed him the glass.

"Thank you very much," I said, taking the package and my bag from the seat next to the one I had sat on.

I was afraid to go outside, although I doubted that the rapist would be waiting for me. But perhaps he knew that I had reported what he had done to me and realized very well that the police would never arrest him even if he did it again. But I couldn't give that any more thought. If I did, I would just end up wetting myself again.

Heading for the door, I put on my sunglasses. I hurried down the street and back to the hotel. I realized that, just like the rape, I would have to try to pretend that this incident hadn't happened either. I glanced at my watch. Two more hours of work and I could call it a day.

***

The nurse at the doctor's office had recommended that I go to a self–help group, but because of my irregular working hours at the hotel that was not possible. Even if I had been able to rearrange my work schedule, however, there was another reason I couldn't go and that was because I felt so guilty. I thought that if I told my story to a group of girls whose rapes might have been brutal and had left them seriously injured, they might say I was to blame for what had happened to me. I guess I didn't think what I had gone through was bad enough compared to what I imagined others had had to endure. My vision of a typical rape scene was one that took place in a dark alley and involved an attack by a vicious criminal. The person who had done this to me had appeared to be an ordinary man, and it had happened in my apartment. I had even let him in. How could I say all of that in front of other victims and expect any understanding? I didn't have any bad injuries to prove that anything had happened. But a lot had. I knew, even then, that I would never be the same.

I was scared and, at the same time, I felt dirty and embarrassed. I didn't want anyone to know that this had happened to me.

And I was angry with the police for not helping me more. But I didn't know where else to go or what to do. I was in a foreign country and wasn't familiar with the customs or the law. It was quite a challenge for me to stay abroad, far away from my friends and family. But I finished the eight–month term of my contract, trying to pretend that the rape had never happened, because it was the only way I saw possible of making it through those following months. I didn't tell anyone. It was just my secret, one I tried very hard to ignore and forget.

Chapter 2

"So," my plump, bespectacled eleventh–grade chemistry teacher asked me, "have you looked into any good schools?"

I knew my teachers expected me to go to some prestigious college. I was bright, diligent and committed, and I had always been a good self–motivator.

"I'm looking," I replied, fidgeting with my pencil case, trying to avoid his glance.

"You could always become a lawyer or a doctor, you know," he added.

Weren't there enough lawyers and doctors out there yet? Why did the world need another one?

I remembered my biology teacher telling me, only the week before, that I should never become a surgeon. We had been dissecting a cow's eye, and I'd had such a hard time removing the lens.

"Press down on it hard," my friend Jacky had called out to me.

When I did, the lens suddenly flew out, and I had to spend quite some time looking for it on the dark–colored carpet.

No, I would certainly not become a doctor, and I thought I would find law boring. Much to the disapproval of my teachers I had decided not to apply to a school just yet. Instead, since I had always wanted to go abroad, I decided to do some traveling after high school. The extra language courses I had taken in school would make it easier to travel. And, since Auntie Rosalie was from the French–speaking part of Switzerland, she mostly spoke French to Nicholas and me. As a result, Spanish and Italian had not required that much effort to learn. I wanted to get out there in the world, and I couldn't wait.

Although I was born in Switzerland, I had grown up on the East coast, moving in with Auntie Rosalie, my mother's sister, Uncle Stephen and Cousin Nicholas after my parents were killed in a car accident when I was about a year old.

My tall, deep–voiced, fat–bellied uncle was employed by a multinational as their finance manager. At home, just as at work, he expected people to do as they were told, even Auntie Rosalie. I never thought of Uncle Stephen as a happy man since the only emotions he ever showed were anger, disappointment and disapproval. And he was always formal, even wearing white shirts and dress trousers at home.

My aunt, a slender, attractive woman who looked a great deal younger than my uncle, perhaps because of the quantity of beauty products she bought, worked part–time as an administrative assistant for a local realtor.

Although I saw much less of Nicholas since he'd begun studying science at the University of Syracuse, this tall, slender figure with spiky brown hair was still my best friend.

The four of us, joined by our playful cat, Pearl, had lived in the four–bedroom house on Greenwich Avenue for as long as I can remember.

We were raised Catholic, and since both my aunt and uncle came from traditional Catholic families, we went to church every Sunday. That was not negotiable. Nor were a lot of other things. Auntie Rosalie and Uncle Stephen were strict and didn't put up with any nonsense. Their coldness didn't have anything to do with the fact that I was not their biological daughter, since they treated their own son, Nicholas, who was four years older than I, the same way. Nicholas and I had to be well–behaved and strong from day one. Crying was considered a sign of weakness and apart from the obligatory kiss goodnight, my aunt and uncle were not very affectionate. I was grateful for Pearl, who adored to be cuddled, and my grandparents, Auntie Rosalie's mother and father, who usually came to visit us for a month once a year. When they did they overwhelmed us with warm embraces and presents.

According to my grandparents, as well as my aunt and uncle, marriage was sacred. We were often made to listen to the outrageousness of people who changed spouses as often as they changed shoes. And naturally, as we were Catholic, premarital sex was looked down on.

By the time I was eighteen, my craving to see the world was hard to control. There were so many places I wanted to visit, so many cultures to explore. The books on art history that I had read had opened up an entire new world for me. I wanted to go to Mexico to discover the Mayan culture. And to Peru to learn about the Incas. I was going to climb the Machu Picchu at some point in my life. The temples and pyramids of Egypt were awaiting my visit.

And then I found work in the Caribbean. It was via an advertisement in the paper. I applied and was invited for an interview in May. When I told Auntie Rosalie the good news that I was going to be interviewed, she was excited, too. She knew that I really wanted this. And it seemed like the perfect opportunity to see the world. But when I told her I had to meet a man in a hotel, she warned me not to go to a room with him. I thought she was making a big fuss out of nothing since I knew that it was common practice for job interviews to take place in hotel conference rooms. But she was not convinced and insisted on driving me there. While I went inside, she waited in the car and read the book she had brought to keep her occupied.

The ground–level hotel with what looked like a recently mowed lawn in front had a brick facade with many arches. I walked into the spacious reception area where red armchairs had been placed in clusters around glass tables. The receptionist was wearing a red uniform, which looked quite pretty on her.

"How can I help?" she asked.

"Hi, my name is Elize Carlier. I'm here for a job interview at two with a representative of Carib Resorts. I'm a —"

"Oh, yes," she interrupted me. "You can wait here until he's finished with the candidate he's seeing now. He'll come out here to meet you when he's done. Would you like something to drink?"

Soon after one of the waiters had brought me the glass of sparkling water I'd asked for, the interviewer approached me, carrying several files.

Mr. Sarnell was a stiff–looking fellow of about fifty. His body seemed to be so inflexible I was afraid he'd break something just by sitting down at the conference table in the meeting room he had led me to. But, of course, he did manage to sit down all right on the chair opposite me. He folded his arms on the table and smiled.

"I'm Elize," I began. "I'm here for the interview for the position of receptionist at one of your hotels in the Caribbean, where I would be responsible for checking guests in and out, booking extra nights, answering and transferring calls, handling room keys, assisting clients with all sorts of queries and passing these on to housekeeping, the food and beverage manager, the general management —"

"Right," he said, cutting me off whilst examining my application papers. "Why don't I start by explaining to you what kind of company we are and what kind of people we're looking for? Our company owns several hotels in the Caribbean," he began slowly in a deep voice. "We're not a chain. The hotels are run independently, but all of them maintain the same standards. We are looking for several staff members at various hotels. They may spend some time at one hotel and then move to another, so it is necessary for everyone we hire to be extremely flexible. Is that a problem for you?"

"No, of course not," I said, excited by the thought that this job might take me to several islands. "That's absolutely fine."

"Good," he said. "I'm glad to hear that. You've applied for a position as a receptionist, I see."

"Yes," I said. "I enjoy having direct contact with people, and I think I am very customer oriented. I organize well, I can multi–task, and I work well under pressure."

"You're a bit young, aren't you?" he said. "You don't have any real experience."

"I know," I said. "But I'm very keen to learn and very determined to do well. And I'm motivated. I really want this job."

"I can see that," Mr. Sarnell said. "Now tell me about other international experiences you've had. I want to be sure you won't get homesick after the first week."

I told him how fascinated I had been by my trip to France, which I had undertaken independently. I also mentioned that I had traveled to Switzerland two years earlier, although I didn't mention that I had gone with Nicholas and that it had been to visit our grandparents.

"Yes, but have you ever been to South America or Central America or, more importantly, the Caribbean?" he asked. "It's very different from Europe, you know."

I admitted that I hadn't but went on to compensate by explaining that I had read a lot about other cultures because they had always fascinated me and that I spoke other languages. I was determined to ace this interview and just as determined that, if he hired me, it would be a decision he would not regret.

***

Since the position in the Caribbean wouldn't be open until October, Mr. Sarnell had said he might not get back to me until the end of the summer. But wanting this job as badly as I did, I followed up with him regularly.

After graduation I worked in a supermarket, filling up shelves to earn extra cash, and, a few weeks later, I took on a second job checking invoices. I had my mind set on traveling, so if I didn't get the job I would certainly need the money. And if I did get it I would save the money for a future trip. I wanted to see the world. I was merely starting out with the Caribbean.

In September Mr. Sarnell called me to ask me if I was still interested in working in the Caribbean. And, of course, I was. The thought crossed my mind that perhaps he was so fed up with hearing from me that he just decided to give me a go.

I was ecstatic but apprehensive at the same time since I had never actually worked abroad, and the fact that I had never been to the Caribbean made me feel additionally apprehensive.

Once the decision had been made, there was no turning back. Some of my friends were happy for me and supportive, even a little envious. Others thought I was crazy and told me they would never dare to do anything like that.

The company was going to call me and give me a reservation number so that I could pick up my ticket at the airport. Mr. Sarnell had told me that I would first be trained at one particular hotel and only afterward find out where I would be working. When the company actually called me to confirm the exact date of my flight, I was all set to head for my Caribbean extravaganza even though all I knew about what would happen on my arrival was that someone would pick me up at the airport and take me to my accommodation.

I had bought some books about the islands, but had no time to do any reading. I thought I might do it on the plane. Of course, I didn't.

Actually, I was exhausted, mainly from not having taken a break after high school graduation. And then I had worried about Nicholas, who had fallen off a ladder while helping a friend do some outside painting. I asked him if he wanted me to stay home longer, to postpone the trip. But he told me he would be fine. A bruised arm and a broken shoulder should not keep me from going he had said, adding that he'd feel guilty if I didn't go because of him.

But I was going to miss Nicholas. I knew that. He had always been there for me. Although he couldn't always be with me physically, in spirit we were always joined.

But after having spent all those years craving adventure, it was time for a change. Of course, I was hoping for a change for the better. But change always meant taking a risk.

So after all the good–byes, all the meetings with friends I wouldn't see for several months, and the last family dinners, I was all set. The whole family, Auntie Rosalie, Uncle Stephen and even Nicholas, went to the airport with me. It was the first time I had planned to be away from home for such a long time, and, although I was overjoyed to be going on this adventure, I knew I would be missing out on all the things that would happen here during the eight months that I was away.

At the airport the check–in agents told me I had brought too much luggage and at first refused to accept it. I was not amused. Somehow the problem was resolved. And finally I was off.

***

The Caribbean airport was tiny and not crowded at all, so I immediately identified the skinny lady who had come to pick me up. She was holding two signs, one of which had my name on it, and was wearing a dark blue, woolen skirt and jacket, a uniform that seemed totally out of place in such a warm climate. But this native lady, who I guessed to be in her mid–forties, was lively and enthusiastic.

I walked up to her. "Hi," I said, "I'm Elize, a new employee."

"Nice to see you," she replied enthusiastically, swinging the signs back and forth.

I almost ducked. I didn't want to make a bad impression, but I didn't want to be knocked out either.

"How was your flight?" she asked me, and then added, without waiting for a reply, "We're still expecting another new employee to arrive. He's on the same flight."

"All right," I said. "I'll just wait here until he comes."

"Have a seat," she said. "It could be a while."

I sat down although that was the last thing I wanted to do having spent all that time on a plane.

I had seen the overweight, tousled–haired young man who came walking toward us now on the plane earlier and had thought he looked the friendly type.

"Hi, I'm Elize," I said. "I think we're part of the same training program."

"I'm glad I'm not the only one," James told me as we carried our luggage. It turned out that he came from Boston, and that this was his first time out of the country. The impression I got from James that day was that he seemed to be withdrawn, but perhaps I was wrong and he was merely exhausted from the trip and therefore didn't feel like talking much.

"This is the one," the lady from the transportation company said as we reached a white town car. "I just dropped off some tourists. Their adventure ended and yours is about to begin." She gave a quick grin, although she had made it all sound a bit ominous.

It was obvious that she was quite a character, clearly proud to be so neatly dressed in her blue uniform, and not at all adverse to speaking her mind.

"Let's go," she shouted, flinging open the back door after having stowed our luggage in the trunk.

Once we were on our way, her monologue began. And her high–pitched voice made her unpleasant to listen to.

"So how do you like your new home?" she asked. "You know, I've been driving for these hotels for fifteen years. It's always the same. People come and go. I should leave too. We local people aren't paid too well, you know. And your boss, he's a peculiar fellow, all right."

James and I exchanged looks. It was clear that we were on the same wavelength here.

"You know," she continued, "I only found out yesterday I had to do this shift. They always let me know the very last minute. You can't plan anything that way. They don't let me have a life. Now Maria, who also does these shifts, she's really been taken advantage of. She always changes her plans at the very last minute if they call her for a

35

shift and never complains. Never. She's afraid to. She's a sucker. I wouldn't let that happen to me."

I stopped listening as we drove toward our hotel that was located in the northern bay area. Leaving the airport, we had passed the ruins of a restored fortress, which hinted at the military history of the island. The weathered houses with wooden shutters and hanging plants were soon replaced by stucco buildings in every pastel color imaginable. The island seemed to be one enormous tropical garden with fruit–bearing trees, brightly colored hibiscus, wild orchids and many other exotic flowers. Each new beauty spot I saw made me want to see more.

We drove alongside a strip of brilliant white sand and passed several water sports centers. I wanted to learn how to sail, windsurf, water–ski and scuba dive so that I could discover the coral reefs this tropical paradise had to offer. I relished the thought of swimming in these clear blue waters and sunbathing on the beaches. Intrigued by everything I saw through the car window, I knew I had definitely come to the right place.

Our trip led us past several luxurious beach resorts. They looked exactly like the pictures I had seen in the brochures I had picked up at a local travel agency back home. One of the hotels, I noticed, had a golf course with water holes lined with coconut palms, well–tended tennis courts, and I imagined there to be the sort of spectacular swimming pool, complete with waterfall and swim–up bar in the back that I remembered from the pictures in the travel brochures. Another was an equally impressive Mediterranean–type beachfront resort, set amid exotic palm–shaded gardens with cobblestone walkways and brilliantly colored bougainvillea everywhere. And there were stucco seafront cottages painted in soft pastels, as well. All in all, this island seemed to be a perfect Garden of Eden.

About twenty–five minutes later, the lady pulled up to a stylish–looking hotel with white iron balconies and a pastel blue facade accented by flower boxes. "This is your stop," she bellowed. "There are several shops here within walking distance, if you need anything, and there's a splendid panoramic view of the town and harbor up there," she added, pointing up the corkscrew road, "if you're willing to do the climb. It's well worth it."

But we were both tired from the flight. "Maybe some other time," we chorused.

"Tomorrow morning you're both expected at the Four Winds Hotel just down the road here," she went on, taking our luggage out of the trunk. "It's about a twenty–minute walk. Be there nine a.m. sharp. Have a good night's rest."

"Thank you! Bye–bye!" we shouted as she drove off.

The Palm Hotel was built in colonial style and surrounded by lush, tropical gardens. The reception area was decorated in pastel colors with island motifs. After filling in some forms at the reception desk, I carried my bags upstairs to my simply furnished new room with its jaunty blue and white striped curtains that matched the bedspreads. Unable to wait to get my feet wet in the beckoning blue sea, I rushed back down to the inviting turquoise waters that lapped against the white sand of a long, narrow beach. After a casual barefoot stroll, I went to bed early, exhausted from the trip.

On our drive from the airport, I had discovered that James seemed to know even less about the job than I did.

The next morning he and I headed for the Four Winds Hotel where we would get our initial training. The reception area of this hotel was bright with colors reflecting the corals of the sea. As we walked down the corridors, I glanced into the open rooms that were being cleaned. Decorated in island pastels and with terrazzo floors, these king size rooms had ceiling fans, telephones, radios and satellite TV. Plants rimmed the balconies and white drapes covered the louvered windows.

Our Caribbean boss, a brisk man in his mid–thirties who had a picture of his wife and young daughter on his cluttered wooden desk, briefly explained that we would be trained at the Four Winds Hotel for two weeks before being appointed to a particular hotel to work in. He then went over company policies and our training program.

After a three–hour meeting, James and I made our way back to the reception, passing a twisting, white stairway and taking a peek into the inside dining room, furnished in traditional colonial style with plank floor and mahogany tables. The louvered doors opened to the alfresco garden extension with flowering pink, orange and yellow shrubs. In the distance I heard the rhythmic crashing of the waves on the shore. This dazzling place I would call work for the next two weeks.

In the afternoon we were free to do what we wanted. Get some rest. Acclimatize. The company had deliberately let us stay at a different hotel from the one we'd be trained at in order to give us more privacy and to ensure we would not be mixing with guests in our spare time. Once we were given a particular hotel to work in, after the training, we would be allocated private accommodation.

We spent that afternoon on the hotel beach, lying in hammocks that had been strung between two palms, getting a head start on our tan. This was the life.

But we still had to become acquainted with the area. So the following day, James and I were scheduled to go on a discovery tour of the island together. James was a quiet fellow, about my height, not very energetic in nature, and inclined to keep to himself. But I soon figured out that he would be a good friend. What you told him he kept to himself. This fair–skinned, brown–haired, clumsy–looking individual had a good heart. He and I got on well, particularly since he was also very interested in culture and history.

The outing was indeed a true discovery. I was overcome with sheer amazement by the splendor of the fauna and flora this island had to offer. There were dense rainforest and crystal clear lagoons, not to mention the scrumptious cuisine based on plentiful supplies of lobster, shrimp, coconuts, tropical fruit and spices. This was heaven. It was all too good to be true, as I would learn later on.

But for the present I could scarcely believe that I was living this life: being greeted by the Caribbean sun everyday; waking up to the smell of the freshness of the plants; basking in the clear blue waters; and relaxing on spectacular beaches cooled by the gentle trade winds. It was paradise.

***

Two weeks later, James and I moved out of the Palm Hotel. I was given an apartment in St. Catherine's, a small town at the southern end of the island, within walking distance from my job at the equally glorious Primrose Hotel with a gated entry and handcrafted interiors of natural woods. This estate featured an upscale dining area, a fitness center with saunas, a beauty parlor, a rejuvenating spa, a lagoon–style pool with a cascading waterfall, superb tennis facilities, tropical gardens with colorful flowers and towering palms, and an onsite water sports center on the crescent–shaped shore provided an array of fun–filled activities. The hotel suites offered private patios or balconies with either a sea or garden view.

Leaving the luxuries of a top–notch hotel behind, I settled in to my fully furnished, ground–floor apartment with a fitted kitchen and a white tiled bathroom. The thick brick walls of the living room were tastefully decorated with some colorful paintings.

James was appointed to a different hotel in the northern bay area and shared an apartment with Jake, a student from Michigan who had arrived a few weeks earlier.

It was now the period between the summer and winter season, and I was glad not having to spend another cold winter at home. I was happy that I had decided to come here and was certain that many of my friends back home envied my life on this tropical island.

***

My Caribbean adventure hadn't even lasted two months when it happened. That morning I had called to have my sink fixed and the man I had spoken with on the phone had told me someone would come by between five and six that evening. I was at home in my apartment in St. Catherine's at about five forty–five, after having returned from an early shift, when he arrived with his toolkit. As I let him, I realized that I had seen him before at the hotel. He was a tall, brown–eyed, dark–haired, dark–skinned man, who was dressed in dungarees and a T–shirt. He had broad shoulders and his chin had a dark–colored birthmark on it. He may have come to fix the pipes, but I soon realized that he had other interests. And by that time it was too late.

What do I remember?

I let him in and showed him the way to the kitchen sink, which he needed to repair.

"This is the one that needs to be fixed," I said. "When I turn the water on it works fine for a while, but then water just starts leaking out down here and floods my apartment."

After taking a look under the sink, he took out his tools, and I left the kitchen in order not to get in his way. I had just picked up the book I had been reading, when I heard him packing up. Putting the book back down, I headed for the door so that I could show him out. But he blocked my way and shoved me so hard that I almost lost my balance.

"What do you think you're doing?" I shouted.

He came toward me and pushed me face forward against the wall.

"Get off me!" I yelled. "Get the hell off me!"

He pressed so hard against me that I could not move, pulling at my clothes. He was too heavy for me to push away. "Stop! Stop!" I begged him over and over again.

I had begun to cry.

He pressed my face against the wall and pulled down the sweatpants I had changed into after work, as well as my underwear. All the time he was leaning against me.

"I don't want to do this," I cried. "Let me go!"

He entered my body.

"Stop! Please don't do this to me! Please stop!" I begged.

He was inside me, inside the place I had managed to keep private for so many years. He had no right. Didn't he care how precious this was to me? And the pain was excruciating. It felt as though he were tearing me open inside.

"Let me go!" I cried again. "You can't do this to me!"

And although I continued to beg him to stop, he didn't.

He made me wash myself and left me in the bathroom. And then he had left, taking so much of me with him. What did I have left now? I had never felt so filthy in my entire life. And I felt completely helpless. I wrapped myself in a towel and crawled out to the other room, feeling weak and sick, and dropped to the floor.

I lay there for a long time, pulling at the tear–drenched carpet. This could not have happened. I closed my eyes tight, hoping that when I opened them again it would all just be a bad dream. But it wasn't.

Chapter 3

"Just give a yell if you guys want to stop for a picture," the bearded, laid–back French tour guide clad in ripped blue denims and a loose white shirt shouted to us in the back of the minibus. "You don't let me know, I don't stop. No pictures, right?"

"Right," we all shouted back at him.

There were eight of us, a tiny group: a Canadian student and her mother; two German girls in their mid–twenties; a British couple, who I guessed to be in their thirties; a middle–aged Swedish biologist who kept very much to himself and me. It was a cozy little group.

The minibus had come to pick us up early that morning for an excursion to the Lubéron range and the Parc Naturel Régional du Lubéron. The European soil I had escaped to was real, but freedom was a mere illusion.

That same morning I had made my bed in the dorm room of the Avignon hostel I was staying at. After having tucked in the sheets on the other side of the bed I turned to back out of the tiny gap between the bed and the wall. And there I stood, faced with the wall again. Standing with my face so close to any wall had made me tremble ever since the incident in the Caribbean. I quickly moved sideways out of the gap between the wall and the bed, deciding I'd leave the sheets hanging out on that side from now on. Anything to keep the brown–eyed Caribbean monster with the dark–colored birthmark and arrogant smile from appearing before me.

The tall blond Swede yelled, "Stop Vincent, I want a picture here," and the minibus pulled over. We all got off to admire the splendid view of the hills and pretty villages. Yes, the Provence was stunningly beautiful.

I had returned from the Caribbean at the end of May and taken about three months off. My contract would be renewed, and at my request I'd be working in a hotel on a different island. I was glad about that.

I had first flown home to have my HIV test done, which luckily turned out to be negative. It had now been six months and I could finally get on with my life, I thought. The whole experience could just be something I could erase from my life. There would be no permanent damage — I thought then — as I hadn't become pregnant and hadn't caught any diseases. I was actually quite tired from working abroad and needed a holiday.

But the real reason I was traveling was because I couldn't be home, since I didn't want to tell my family about the assault. A huge wall had been erected between them and me, and I was too weak to break it down. In the short time that I spent with my family after returning from the Caribbean, my moods already annoyed them: I was hypersensitive and not at all cheerful. Being there with them had been so painful that I had no choice. I had to leave, although I felt as though I were being banished from my home.

In an attempt to compensate for my loss, I decided to return to my roots and spent about two weeks with my grandparents in Lausanne after which I had continued my trip through France. But during my visit with them the relationship I had with my grandmother was affected by the attack. I spent a lot of time in their spare room crying because I was stuck with the secret I couldn't tell anyone about. But I had reading books with me and told them that I was upset because of the tragedy of the stories I read. I realized it had especially offended my grandmother. She was right there and yet so far away, just as my family in the States had been.

My trip would last for about eight weeks, starting out in Switzerland and continuing through the south of France and Spain. But now that I was there, I was faced with the bitter reality. I couldn't get the incident out of my mind. The rapist continued to haunt me all over Europe.

Even now he stood there next to me, admiring the view, and when I walked to the other side of the minibus, he followed. His arrogance made me sick. I was trapped. I wondered if I was more vulnerable because I was on holiday and not working. Now I had the time to think. Even though I had a busy schedule, visiting places, going on tours, traveling from one place to the other, the rape and the man who had done it preoccupied my mind. No matter where I was, or what I was doing, I felt his presence. He had sat beside me on the train from Lausanne, he had strolled along as I smelled the various aromas at the perfumeries in Grasse, and he had accompanied me on my visit to the Museum of Modern and Contemporary Art in Nice. It was this being that wouldn't leave my side. His face would appear before my eyes and the image would not let me go.

That evening the minibus dropped us off at the hostel again. It had been a marvelous excursion. I found the south of France to be one of the most wonderful places I'd ever been to. But my mind was not at rest. I was not at peace with myself. I tipped the driver, thanked him and followed the others into the hostel.

I walked over to the reception area to pick up my key. The brochures had now been replenished, and a green pamphlet caught my eye. I picked it up. "Sex against your will is rape and it's a crime," I read. I took some of the other brochures, too, so that, if anyone were watching, it wouldn't look like I was only taking that one. This secretiveness was something new for me, still another way that the rape had changed my life.

Up in my dorm room the three Australian girls I was sharing with were getting ready to go out.

"How was your trip?" Sally asked me, as she searched her backpack.

"It was great. Beautiful views," I said, checking to make sure that the green pamphlet was covered by the other brochures I was holding. "Where are you guys off to?" I asked, merely out of politeness, but not at all interested.

"Just dinner," she said. "Do you want to come?"

"No, I'm all right," I told her. "We stopped to eat somewhere along the way."

"All right, maybe some other time," she said, continuing to get her things together to go shower.

"Sure," I said and went to lie down on my bed. It was the last time the sheets would be tucked in this well, while I was there at least.

I wasn't being a loner. I did plenty of socializing. I would even spend some time with friends in Toulouse. But right now, I wanted to read the pamphlet.

Holding one of the larger brochures behind the pamphlet so that no one could see it, I began to read. The section about what you should do to avoid being raped included advice about avoiding deserted areas, walking and jogging alone, drinking from a glass that might have been tampered with when you were in a public place, etc. Further down on the page I read that many people were raped by someone they knew, and that it could happen to anyone. The pamphlet also mentioned that even if you showered, evidence could still be found and therefore it was still worthwhile to go see a doctor. I hadn't known that. I had just been to see the doctor to make sure I hadn't caught anything. At the bottom there was a number to call if it happened to you or if you knew it had happened to someone else.

The following morning I got up, got dressed, washed and headed for the store, wearing suntan lotion, a hat and sunglasses, all bare necessities in this blazing heat. I felt the heaviness of the climate weigh on me from the minute I left the hostel. It was only a fifteen–minute walk to the store. But I was not alone. Beside me on my left was the despicable Caribbean with the grimace on his face. He had come along for free. Although he was taller, his eyes always met mine. If I turned to the right I felt his eyes dig into me. If I turned to the left, wishing he too would turn that way, his smirking face looked right back at mine. Was he telling me I could run, but never hide? In the Caribbean I had been afraid of accidentally meeting him, but as long as we were on the same island I suppose he felt he still had a grip on me, even though he was not by my side. Now that I had left the island he would have to be beside me always to ensure I did not forget. And I didn't. Not for a split second. He was now my dark unwanted companion who would never leave my side. Sometimes I dressed him in jeans and a T–shirt, other times in work trousers and a collared top. Today I even noticed his scraped elbow. Although a figment of my imagination, he was all too real.

I had shut the experience out for many months, pretending it had never happened. Now I was dealing with the consequences. I never summoned him, but he was always present.

After having wandered about the walled city of Avignon for most of the day, I returned to the hostel. My feet were sore, even though I had worn comfortable running shoes. I went upstairs, removing them as I entered the room. Just about to throw them in the direction of my bed, I noticed Sally sitting on the floor next to her locker. There were four metal lockers in the room, one for each bed. But each of us had her own lock. Sally always seemed to be taking things out of her big black backpack and then putting things back in. At least that is what I saw her doing most of the time.

"You look tired," she said as I threw myself on the bed.

"I am," I replied. "My feet are killing me."

"Do you want to join us for dinner tonight?" she asked me.

"Sure," I said, in need of more distraction. "Sounds great."

"We'll be leaving at about eight," Sally said. "Can you be ready by then?"

I looked at my watch. It was six fifteen. "I think I can manage," I replied.

How much time did she think I needed? A quick shower and a short snooze, or at least some time with my feet up, would be enough.

And indeed, after a short rest on my bed, the numbness in my feet was replaced with some sensation. These tingling appendages would soon be as good as new.

I could recover quickly from my physical exhaustion, but also mentally I was worn out and I was hoping that a night out with the girls would cheer me up and enable me to relax.

The four of us, Sally, Samantha, Caroline and I, grabbed a bite to eat at a bar. Since all of us were cheapskates, we deliberately chose one of the places we had coupons for from the hostel. The three girls were students at the James Cook University in Townsville where Sally and Caroline were majoring in psychology and Samantha was studying law.

There was nothing fancy about the place we had chosen. They served alcohol, but being in France, we were not asked for ID. We sat down at a wooden table with wooden benches on each side, just like at the hostel. After having stuffed ourselves with a green salad, quiche Lorraine and a variety of French cheeses, and casually talking about our travels, some new arrivals demanded our attention.

Two guys in their early twenties joined us. They had just walked over and sat down on the benches beside us, one next to Sally and one next to Samantha on the other side. They were British, both casually dressed in cotton trousers and T–shirts.

I was glad to be sitting a bit further away. Ever since the rape I couldn't stand it when men gave me much attention. It made me feel unsettled and unwell. I just wanted to be left alone. When the incident had happened, I had weighed about 105 pounds. But after the attack, I just ate and ate. As a consequence, I had put on weight and found myself to be less attractive to men, which made me feel safer. I was so offended when a man took an interest in me that I went out of my way to make sure that didn't happen very often. But when it did, I showed my worst side to ensure he would lose interest almost immediately. It genuinely upset me to be bothered by a man. I was just afraid. I didn't trust any of them. Too bad for the ones with honorable intentions. I could not afford to take the risk of making a mistake in judgement.

The other girls flirted with the guys, but I didn't find them attractive. They were both seriously overweight, loud, ill–mannered and arrogant. Had they asked to sit down? No. They had just taken it for granted that we wouldn't mind their joining us and proceeding to slurp their beer.

"So, where are you from?" Samantha asked, clearly eager to start some kind of conversation.

"We're from England," one of them replied. "How about yourselves?"

"Australia," Sally said.

"You both are?" the other guy asked.

Sally and Samantha nodded. I guess that meant that Caroline and I were going to be ignored.

"I need to go to the restroom," Caroline said.

"I'll go with you," I said, not wanting to be left sitting there.

When we got back, Sally and Samantha had clearly loosened up. In fact, they were all over the two guys, stroking their arms and backs, cuddling up to them, and laughing loudly.

"I don't want to go sit with them," Caroline said to me. "Let's go dance."

I agreed, and we worked our way between the crowd and into a little open space with just enough room for us to move.

When I was in junior high school, my aunt had agreed to let me visit Linda, a friend from school, who was spending the summer at her parents' beach house in the south of France, as long as I paid for the trip by taking a job for the first part of the summer. When I arrived in France, I discovered that Linda's brother, Jeff, and his friend Sam had also decided to spend a few days there. We mainly hung out at the house and, of course, went to the beach.

One evening we had decided to go to a nearby steakhouse. After having given the food some time to digest, we headed for a club that was about a thirty–minute drive from the restaurant. Even then we hadn't been asked for ID. We all ordered at the bar, although I just had a soda, not wanting to risk the effect even one drink might have on me.

Linda and I had wanted to go dance. The place wasn't that big, so it easily got crowded and people were basically dancing everywhere they could find some space to move. The music was very loud inside. Linda and I did our thing: a routine that was not supposed to look like one but that kept us going for a while. We must have looked odd, but we had fun. We were giggling and so caught up in our own moves that we hadn't noticed this guy, probably in his early twenties, dancing right beside us. Suddenly he spoke.

"Do you want to dance with me?" he asked me.

He spoke English, too, although, based on his accent, I couldn't tell where he was from. He was wearing ripped jeans and a T–shirt. As far as I was concerned, he was just a regular guy.

Linda pushed me. "Go on," she said to me, and then to him, "She'd love to."

"Sure," I said a little hesitantly.

It was all right at first. But suddenly the boy I was dancing with moved closer and started to kiss my neck.

"Stop that!" I told him.

I tried to pull away, but he wouldn't let me go. I couldn't see Linda.

"I'm with a friend, remember?" I said. "She's waiting for me. I have to go."

"I don't believe you," he said, pursuing me further. He came closer with his body and mouth to kiss me once again. I was horrified.

"I want you to stop!" I cried. "Let me go!"

I was yelling at the top of my voice. And I was crying. I guess the music must have been on too loud for anyone to hear. I was terrified that I might fall to the floor. There he would be able to do with me what he wanted. I had to stay standing which wasn't so easy because I was struggling and he was clamping himself to me. Also, I realized he was drunk. Finally, I managed to pull myself away from him. I ran outside, pushing everyone I passed to the side, determined to get out.

Linda came running after. She had been standing near the entrance and had seen me rush out like a madwoman. She grabbed me, and I held on to her tight. My eyes were pouring. I was so scared. I just wanted to go home and never go to a place like that again.

"What happened?" she asked. "I thought you were fine, so I went to stand by the door. I'm so sorry. I should have stayed with you."

Linda knelt beside me. Through my tears I saw the concern on her face. Her mouth had opened slightly, and the worried look in her eyes made me feel like a child. I tried to pull myself together.

"I just want to go home," I said. "He wouldn't let me go. I just want to go home."

"All right," she said in a soothing voice. "I'll go get the others."

She gave me a tight squeeze and then went back to get Jeff and Sam. As we drove back to the beach house I remember thinking that someone could easily be raped in a place like that and no one would do anything! Nobody would notice or pay any attention to it. What a scary thought. It made me shiver and sent chills down my spine.

Perhaps it was being in France once again that made me remember that night. I suppose it's all very well, having a prescription of what you need to do to avoid being sexually assaulted, taking the kind of steps the pamphlet had mentioned, but no matter how careful a woman is, she can still be accosted, anywhere and anytime, and probably more often than you care to believe in places which would appear to be very safe.

That night we stayed until about one. The girls had booked an excursion for the following day that would include the cities of Nîmes and Arles and the Camargue wetlands. We walked back to the hostel, in part to sober Sally and Samantha up, just the three girls, me and the dark–haired broad–shouldered man who had raped me, the man who never seemed to leave my side.

That was my fate in France. Although I had intended to travel alone, that would never be an option again. First the rapist had forced himself into my body, and now he had forced himself into my mind, my eyes, my ears. I could even smell him. This was my life now. Although fundamentally alone, I would forever be joined.

***

I continued my journey through the south of France to Spain, where I met the same fate. I heard the phrase *es una chica muy triste* as I paid for my bus ticket, as I strolled past the shops and as I admired a painting in one of the museums. Although I could take in everything I saw and heard around me, the only thing I could let out were tears. They hinted at the bottled up feelings inside, as they poured down my cheeks continually.

I visited Andalusia, a region with a rich cultural heritage, and I think the Alhambra in Granada dazzled me the most. Thanks to the art history books I'd read, I had acquired an insatiable interest in old buildings, paintings and sculptures, and, because of what I had learned from them, I also found myself looking at art work in a very different way, trying to remember which styles of architecture and which ornaments and features were typical of a particular period in time. These amazing pieces of work such as the archeological site Medina Azahara, the Mosque in Cordoba, and the Cathedral and Alcazar in Seville were all so impressive. Although I felt miserable, I was surrounded by indescribable beauty.

I traveled cheaply, since I took the bus from one place to another and stayed in youth hostels. Very few people spoke English, so my knowledge of Spanish proved to be no luxury.

I was pretending to be this young culturally interested traveler, which in fact I was, but little did anyone know about my dark secret, this dirty clandestine experience I carried around with me everywhere. I'd cry a lot, just walking from one museum to another, anytime the situation got the better of me. But I had sunglasses that I could put on. An easy excuse, which often came in very handy, was that my eyes were teary because of my imaginary contact lenses, or saying that I had a cold or an allergy would do sometimes.

I felt so lost. Why was this happening to me? I thought I'd already dealt with the horror. But now I realized that I hadn't. In fact, I had chosen not to deal with it. I wondered why I had suddenly thought of that time at the club with Linda? Had the harassment by the drunken boy been a sign that I hadn't understood, telling me to be careful? I didn't know.

But there I was, traveling through Spain in tears, living the life of an exile.

Although I think there was one day when I barely cried. It was the day I visited the spectacular hill town Ronda, where the Puente Nuevo, the main bridge that connected the old part of the town with the new, offered breathtaking views of the gorge.

Ronda was crowded, mainly with tourists. I wasn't spending the night there; it was just a quick visit of about four or five hours. During the siesta, when the shops were closed, I strolled from one side of the town to the other, going back and forth between the old part and the new. Both seemed to coexist perfectly. So it was possible to have both.

I became aware that I could still hold on to the old me. I didn't have to let her go after all. Although the two parts of myself could never fully integrate, realizing that I could preserve the eighteen–year–old girl I had once been came as a great relief. She did not have to be dead.

Therefore it is Ronda that I always refer to as the most beautiful town in the south of Spain. Although my ray of hope was very soon covered up by dark, heavy clouds, at least I had seen it then.

***

Immediately after the rape I had felt as though I had lost everything that had been dear to me. I couldn't understand how it could have been possible. It seemed so unreal. Every thought I had was vague. I couldn't grasp that this had happened to me. I suppose I was in shock. I was confused and didn't know what to think or believe.

But very soon I began to feel angry. I was angry with the rapist and with myself: with him, for ruining my life and forcing me into a world of secrecy, lies and loneliness, and with myself, for letting him. If only I had been smart enough to fix that sink myself, I would not have suffered. There could have been a million reasons for not having been alone in my apartment that Friday. Why hadn't I thought of one?

Next to that, I unjustly directed my anger at my family and friends. I was jealous of them for not having to deal with my trauma. It wasn't fair. What had I done to deserve this? And I was angry with them for carrying on with their lives as though nothing had happened. Because that was precisely what I wanted to do, more than anything, but couldn't.

While traveling through Europe I had often experienced shortness of breath. Nothing in particular that I could think of had brought it about, because sometimes I'd had problems breathing shortly after I'd woken up, or late at night before going to bed I'd suddenly begun to gasp for air. At first I'd thought I might just be in bad shape and if I did more physical exercise it might go away. However, it didn't.

As a result, when I returned from Europe, I approached our family doctor. Dr. Campbell was a slim vivacious man in his late thirties or early forties who was mostly dressed in jeans and a sweater.

"Physically, you're fine," he said as he put down his stethoscope and sat down behind his cluttered desk. "You're just hyperventilating," he added with a gentle smile.

I was amazed. He had actually given the phenomenon a name. I had never hyperventilated before, so I didn't know what it was.

Dr. Campbell must have seen the puzzled expression on my face. "It's caused by fear and anxiety," he explained.

And indeed, I certainly knew about those, now. But when my doctor had used these words they hadn't appeared to convey any reason for concern.

"I'm not sleeping well either," I told him, hoping that he would realize that I wasn't all right.

"I understand," Dr. Campbell replied, "but only if you try to relax and deal with the actual cause of it will the hyperventilating stop. Don't look so worried," he added. "If I had just told you that you were terminally ill, you would have the right to put on a face like that. Fretting never helped anyone, so stop!"

He had so many simple answers. And I so badly wanted to confide in him. But I was afraid that he would shrug off what had happened to me on the island as easily as he appeared to be shrugging off my inability to take a breath, my difficulty with sleeping. It seemed clear to me that, when he looked at me, he saw nothing but a healthy young woman. How did I know that, if I told him the truth about what was bothering me, he would offer any sympathy? When I had come for the blood test prior to leaving for Europe, he hadn't asked any questions, probably because he thought I was merely being responsible by being tested. Once again, I decided to just let him believe in his illusion. Mine had already been crushed. There was no point in crushing his, too.

Perhaps because I couldn't find anyone to talk to, I became even more fearful, even in public places, let alone parking lots and areas that I might have understandably felt uncomfortable in. I did carry my cell phone with me all the time and kept it switched on, but I was still worried about not being able to dial or search for the right number straight away. And then, of course, if my attacker saw the cell phone, he would naturally recognize it for what it was and try to take it away from me.

I was so frightened, walking around on my own, that one sunny afternoon, shortly after my doctor's visit, I walked out with my cell phone in one hand and an umbrella in the other.

"You forgot your scarf, hat and rubber boots," Nicholas shouted as I was leaving.

I stopped and felt paralyzed. "What's the matter with you?" he asked, coming after me and taking the umbrella out of my hand. "Why are you carrying this around with you? You know it's not going to rain."

He was clearly making fun of me, and under normal circumstances the whole situation would have been very funny. But to me, nothing that was in any way related to the attack was even remotely humorous.

I was angry, but even more I was afraid. First of all, my umbrella was to serve as a defense aid. But secondly, and more importantly, I didn't want to tell Nicholas about the rape. Maybe if I were just angry with him, he'd feel guilty, get upset and not ask any questions. But I couldn't tell him. Anything was better than that.

"What's your problem anyway?" he asked me, swinging my colorful umbrella around in the air. "Why are you carrying this around with you?"

"Look, if I want to carry it around with me that's my business," I shouted.

"I'm sorry," he said indignantly and handed it back to me.

"Just stay out of my life," I said sharply, trying to end the conversation as quickly as possible so that we could drop the subject and I could stop worrying about him suspecting anything. I knew it had to end before I began crying like a baby.

"I will. I promise," he replied, clearly upset. "I guess you left your sense of humor in the Caribbean." And turning on his heel, he left me.

I was relieved the confrontation was over, but I felt terribly guilty about what I had said to Nicholas. If anything, I wanted him in my life more than ever before. I wanted someone to share this awful secret with. Most of all, I truly wished it had only been my sense of humor that I had left behind in St. Catherine's.

***

A few weeks later I was off to the sun–drenched beaches of a neighboring island where I worked in the seaside town of

Ira, in a sprawling complex a few hundred yards inland from the beach. Rainbow Inn was surrounded by seductive tropical gardens, featuring four outdoor pools, an eighteen–hole golf course, perfectly maintained lighted tennis courts, three restaurants, two bars and a state–of–the–art fitness center.

I thought that going back to work would fix everything. I'd be busy again, and I'd have very little time to be occupied with other thoughts.

And, indeed, getting back to work did help at first. There was a lot to do, new people to meet, new things to learn. The fact that it was a different island did reassure me. I do not think I could have gone back to that same place. However, I was continually looking over my shoulder, terrified of being confronted with the man who had robbed me of my virginity. Although I was able to acknowledge the captivating beauty of the idyllic island, it did not compensate for the terror I held within me.

This time I shared an apartment with Candy, a twenty–one–year–old student from Chicago who was doing her internship for a hotel management course at the same hotel at which I was working. She was tall and thin with bright blue eyes and long sleek blond hair draping down her back. Since she was well aware of her appealing appearance, Candy's attitude was not always easy to put up with. She could have been a model and was always wearing stylish clothes. Having rich parents certainly had its benefits.

She had several boyfriends at a time, desperately looking for a man, one who was willing to give her children, which was surprising because, at first glance, at least, Candy would not have struck anyone as the maternal type. However, she said that she wanted to have at least five children by the time she was thirty, and, since she felt she was running out of time, she said she needed to evaluate more than one candidate at a time. We were about as unlike one another as we could have been, and yet I soon felt that she was a good friend.

Our second–floor apartment was located several blocks from the beach in a built–up area of Ira and was quite large. Although the building wasn't modern, the apartment had been nicely renovated. A new kitchen had recently been installed, the walls were freshly repainted, and new screen doors had been put in. I am a person who needs plenty of sun and, as a consequence, was delighted by the light that poured in through the large windows.

Living and working with me had made it easy for Candy to pick up on my habits and my behavior. She noticed that I was more afraid than she of going outside at night and often joked about me being so worried.

"You're always walking around like a scared little mouse. Are you afraid that maybe you'll be raped?" Candy asked me one evening when we had returned home from work.

I gulped.

She had certainly caught me off guard. We were both standing in the kitchen where I had been cooking my pasta while she prepared her salad. But I was saved by the phone. For the next ten minutes, she chatted with one of her boyfriends.

By the time she returned to the kitchen, I had already taken my pasta with me to my room. I had been lucky not to have to explain. Sitting on my bed, I ate my pasta and kept on eating, although I was crying so hard that my tears dripped into the bowl. I could literally taste my own reality. I was hurting. That much was clear. How much longer could I stand it? How much more could I endure until I broke?

The following week, I wanted to go shopping. When I took my bag and left my room, Candy was standing in the living room.

"Where are you off to?" she asked.

"I'm going shopping," I replied excitedly.

As I was about to turn to head for the door, my eyes caught sight of a headline of the newspaper that was lying on the coffee table. "Senior Citizen Claims Rape," I read.

I felt the blood leaving my face.

"Are you all right?" I heard Candy asking.

"I just need some air," I said.

In shock, I ran for the door and left the apartment in a hurry. Candy's muffled voice followed me down the hallway. I rushed downstairs and opened the front door of the building. A gust of wind blew in my face, although I do not think that was the reason for my tears. They just came pouring out. Fear had got the better of me. Where could I still feel safe? I couldn't go shopping now. Feeling sick I entered the first bar I noticed and spent most of the time in the restroom throwing up.

In fact, that was the beginning of the end. This time I wasn't living alone, but Candy had quite a lot of men over: her boyfriends. I didn't like it. I couldn't lock my room and dreaded the thought of any of them coming in.

A few days later, on my way to the post office, two native men who must have been about my age were ogling and whistling at me. Both were dressed in jeans and tank tops. One had a slender build and was leaning on a parked van. The other stood beside him, holding a skateboard. He was incredibly muscular and could easily have been a bodybuilder. They were calling me, making kissing sounds, and undressing me with their eyes. They followed me for a while, but soon let me be.

But that was the final straw. I was getting out of there. I felt that if I stayed any longer and something happened it would be my fault. I knew that, returning from my job at the hotel, I would often be out late at night. I was petrified. I couldn't eat or sleep. The throwing up, with the addition of diarrhea, just got worse. I couldn't take any more. I just had to leave.

***

Later, having exchanged the warm waters and sun–kissed beaches of the Caribbean for the familiarity of the northern Atlantic coast, I decided to come clean and tell my friend Charlene about the rape. Other than the Caribbean doctor and the police officers, she was the first person I had felt I could tell.

Charlene and I had been close friends since we were only a few years old. If you saw her, you'd think she came straight out of a fairy tale book. She was a year older than I and was known to be the sweetest girl in our village. She was a soft–spoken girl with short blond hair and fair skin. As she was a year older than I, we had never been in the same class at school, but we lived only a few blocks away from each other and often went to a movie together or out for a drink.

Since I had been gone for only about three months — much less than anticipated — she must have suspected at once that something was very wrong. I had sent her an e–mail, saying that I was coming back, and she came over the first Saturday evening after I'd returned. Auntie Rosalie, Uncle Stephen and Nicholas were all out of the house when she arrived.

The first thing she said when she came in was, "I'm thrilled you're back, but weren't you supposed to stay until May? It's only the end of November."

I nodded. Because I had looked away, avoiding her glance, she knew that this was serious. I took her coat and hung it up in the hallway wardrobe. We then sat down on the brown leather sofa in the living room. As Charlene listened to my story, I saw her big blue eyes becoming teary, although I must have sounded vague since my head was a mess. She remained calm, which helped because I was losing it. Someone had to keep it all together. For both our sakes.

At first Charlene had been speechless, aimlessly staring at the wooden coffee table in front of us. She then turned to me and took me in her arms.

After a few minutes Charlene asked me, not loosening her grip, "Didn't your boss ask you any questions? Did he just let you go?" The sound of her voice told me she had been crying.

"I lied to him," I said. "I told him that Auntie Rosalie was sick and that I had to go back home as soon as possible."

"What did he say?" she asked, reaching for a tissue in the pocket of her jeans.

"He said that if I waited until he found a replacement, I could come back," I told her. "But I didn't want to wait. I just wanted to leave straight away."

"Can you go back to work for them later on?" she asked. "You know, when you're, you know…"

"No, but I don't care," I replied.

"What did you tell your aunt?" she asked carefully, her eyes still full of tears.

"I told her it just didn't work out, that I didn't like this island and couldn't be placed back to the other one I was on before."

I saw the hurt and concerned look on Charlene's face and knew she was trying to be supportive.

"I'm really sorry this happened to you," she said as another tear rolled down her cheek.

"Thank you," I said.

Charlene suggested I join a self–help group. But I didn't want to. I had shut the horrible experience out, I thought. Reliving it would not help me. I did still have nightmares, and in the mornings, when I had just woken up, the rapist's face would suddenly appear before me. He was always with me, haunting me everywhere. But, even though it upset me terribly, I felt that a self–help group was more than I could handle.

After that I guess Charlene didn't know what to say. And neither did I. We lay back on the sofa for the remainder of the evening. The things we wanted to say to each other did not require words.

Around eleven o'clock Charlene glanced at her watch and got up. "I have to get going," she said.

I worried if she would be all right. Had I had the right to lay all of that on this sweet, caring girl?

I took her coat out of the wardrobe. She put it on and gave me a tight hug. "Call me if there's anything I can do," she said, closing the door behind her.

I nodded. But even though I knew she cared, I realized that there was nothing she could do.

***

Nicholas had obtained his Bachelor of Science degree from the University of Syracuse and was now working for a French pharmaceutical company in Trenton. But he still lived at home. No one had pressured me to choose a university. I suppose that, since I was the youngest, I had been cut some slack. Nicholas had known what he wanted to do, while I still wasn't sure. I had just wanted to see the world. Perhaps it was also because I'd been working and not just traveling and partying that my aunt and uncle didn't push me much toward getting a degree.

"Do you want to go to the movies with me tonight?" Nicholas asked me several weeks later. The expression on his face implied that I had nothing better to do anyway.

"Sure, I'm bored anyway," I replied, glad that I now had something to do and hoping that the film might offer some distraction.

"You know, two of my friends saw this one film," Nicholas began, getting all excited. "They felt sick for several days after having watched it. In fact, they were both shocked out of their minds."

"And, of course, now you have to see that film, too," I said.

Nicholas smiled and nodded.

"I guess any film will do for me," I replied with a shrug.

The movie began at ten. We went to a theater close by, about a twenty–minute drive from the house. When we arrived, we discovered that, as expected, the film was R–rated. I didn't really care what the movie was about. And as for it having shocked Nicholas' friends, I thought it would have to be quite something in order to shock me. I was more concerned about it being a boring film rather than one that would move me.

We entered the theater at nine forty–five, bought our tickets and went to find a seat. I was surprised so many people had showed up to see the film since Nicholas and his friends quite often had peculiar tastes when it came to entertainment, tastes that were not always shared by many people.

Nicholas always had to sit in the center of the theater because he said he would get a stiff neck from looking over too much to one side, so we sat down in two empty seats near the middle of one of the rows toward the back. After a few commercials, the movie started.

For the first few minutes I was fine. But then it happened. Three female characters in their twenties were out jogging together in the woods in the late afternoon. Suddenly, they were grabbed by five men. The girls were overpowered and then raped, several times. I stopped looking at the screen because it was too painful to watch, but I could still hear what was going on. I wanted to run out of the theater and just keep going. But I just sat tight and let the tears pour out of my eyes until the scene was finally over.

I looked over to Nicholas, but he hadn't noticed me crying. I can't remember why I stayed. Maybe it was because I felt so numb. I couldn't have got up if I had tried.

The remainder of the film contained extremely violent scenes in which the five villains randomly, brutally attacked and mutilated innocent men who were minding their own business in the streets, mostly after the ruffians had taken drugs, and I assumed those were what had shocked Nicholas' friends. But, after having gone through those long, painful minutes of hell, that part didn't have much effect on me.

Although the film didn't devote much viewing time to the raped women, naturally, that was what I was fixated on. And I could relate very well to the three women's hatred, especially toward anything with a penis. I truly hated that thing after the attack on me.

A certain part of the dialogue between the joggers, which I tried to remember in case I was ever attacked again, went something like: *They can only take your body. If you separate it from your mind and soul, then that is all they can take.*

I found out later that it doesn't work that way.

Or, at least, it shouldn't.

Chapter 4

Because the specter wouldn't leave my side and my nightmares were getting worse, I made an appointment with a psychiatrist. I most certainly didn't look forward to seeing him, but I also didn't think I was dealing with the situation very well on my own.

I met with Dr. Malone, the psychiatrist, the following week. If you've ever seen death, then that is what he looked like: pale, thin, and wearing a strangely outdated black suit and bow tie.

His office was dimly lit, and I noticed that the papers on his desk were neatly arranged in piles. There was the smell of a hospital about the office. In fact, everything about the place, including him, was somehow off–putting.

"What's the problem?" he asked me in a firm clear voice that made me shiver. "Why are you here?"

"I was raped," I mumbled hesitantly. The mere sound of that word always made me cringe.

But there was no reaction. Judging from the placid look on Dr. Malone's face, he obviously needed more information.

"So why are you here then?" he asked me in an inquisitive manner. "Which problems do you have?"

I was still puzzled and didn't say anything for a while. Clearly it was my turn to talk as he was waiting and becoming impatient. I hesitated but began to speak.

"I'm afraid now," I said. "I was never afraid before and I want that feeling of confidence back."

He looked me straight in my eyes and leaned forward slightly.

"Being afraid is all right, because it will protect you," he said loudly and slowly. "You shouldn't want to go back to how you were before."

Was that really his answer?

"Is there anything else?" he asked.

I didn't feel comfortable discussing these issues with this man. If he responded that way to all my symptoms I'd rather not hear anything he had to say. But what choice did I have? Who else could I talk to? I couldn't tell Dr. Malone about the specter because I now feared that he might think that I was insane and have me locked up in a psychiatric institution. I wasn't going to take that risk. Instead, I relied on his advice that being afraid would protect me. Therefore I didn't mention the specter. Instead, I decided to talk to Dr. Malone about telling my future fiancé — whoever he might be — about what I had been through.

"Won't he notice?" I asked timidly, sitting rather uneasily on the hard chair in front of his desk. "How can he not notice?"

"Sex is more than a mechanical act," Dr. Malone said. "It is part of the emotional response that two people have for one another."

"But shouldn't I at least tell him?" I asked him rather desperately.

"Why? I see no need to," he replied.

"But then what if it causes problems?" I insisted. How could it not cause problems? I was terrified of having to endure anything even remotely similar to what I had been through.

"If it does, then talk about it," he said with a shrug. "You might not even have to tell him then. If there's a problem, you can simply talk about how you feel. There's no need to go into what happened. Anyway, don't worry about it," he continued, crossing his arms. "When the time comes everything could very well be all right and then you'll have been stressing yourself out over nothing. Worry about it if it ever is a problem."

He nodded as if to stress that I could rely on his advice. But I needed more reassurance than that.

"So you really think it could all still work out?" I asked him. All I truly wanted was for someone to tell me that my life would be all right again. That I would make it through. That there was a fair chance of me being normal even after what I had been through.

"Yes, of course," he said sharply. "It probably won't even be necessary to tell your future fiancé, when the time comes. He won't notice. It's not as though you were wearing a scarlet letter, you know. He won't know whether you're a virgin or not."

But it was because of the rape that I worried. The truth was, having sex was something I was frightened of beyond belief, but at the same time I knew very well that it was inevitable, which is why I kept on telling myself that sex was something completely different. It had to be, or the thought of ever participating in it was more than I could handle.

What I was looking for so desperately was something that could undo the wretched experience that I had endured. Perhaps if I could find someone I wanted to marry, be joined in holy matrimony, I could rectify what had happened. I wanted that so much. Perhaps, once I was married, that monster would leave my side.

"On your way out, make an appointment to come back in two weeks," Dr. Malone said, handing me a prescription for Prozac. "Start taking this in the meantime."

He got up, opened the door for me, and I left.

I was baffled. There I had been, telling him the most intimate, shameful — to me — details of my existence, only to have him suggest that I take Prozac. I was sick for about two weeks after visiting him. I trembled all over and couldn't eat. I just couldn't grasp it. The obvious truth that rape was something that should not be taken all that seriously was too cruel for me to accept. Did he actually think that it had been a minor incident, something that I should not try to make more important than it was? Was I really making a mountain out of a molehill? Maybe it was no big deal. I didn't know what to believe anymore. I felt so confused and so lost. I didn't know where to turn for help. It was all such a big mess. Was I just demanding attention or feeling sorry for myself? I honestly didn't know.

***

When I decided to accept a job in the Mediterranean basin, Charlene must have thought that I was crazy. After the horrifying experience I had been through, I still hadn't had enough. But I couldn't handle staying at home because I never wanted to tell anyone what had happened to me, except for Charlene. I still felt so ashamed and was afraid of my family's reaction were they ever to find out, so I had to leave before anyone became suspicious, especially since the ordeal continued to have such an impact on my everyday life.

Even more than a year after the assault, there were constant reminders. The experience had become a part of me. I carried it around wherever I went. It prevented me

71

from having a normal life. I still felt so guilty about what had happened and had become aware of the fact that ever since the attack, my guilt level could be pushed up easily. The memory of the rape could turn a cozy evening watching television into a difficult confrontation.

One evening, I watched my aunt's favorite soap opera with her. Like most of these programs, it was about several families and their love affairs. On this particular show, one of the characters, a tall muscular man, was holding two girls hostage. The girls made an attempt to escape when they thought he was asleep, but he woke up and they had to fight him off, which they couldn't. The man didn't even have to injure them or hurt them. A bit of shoving around seemed to be enough.

"I cannot believe that two girls can't fight off one man," Auntie Rosalie said. "How can that be? I don't believe it. Surely between the two of them they can knock him out and tie him up, or at least get out of there."

Naturally that upset me. I was very angry with Auntie Rosalie, which wasn't fair, of course, because she had no way of knowing that I had been in a similar situation and that I couldn't protect myself either. In an attempt to defend myself, I tried to explain why the girls couldn't fight him off. "It may look easy," I argued, "but just try moving a man, taller and heavier than you with quite a set of muscles." I certainly couldn't.

Luckily the scene was interrupted by commercials, and, because I couldn't watch any more, I hurried into the kitchen, saying that I was going to fix myself a snack. I felt weak and stupid for not having been able to prevent the rape from happening. But the bottom line was that I just couldn't move him.

Never before had I wanted to forget something so badly. But references to the rape seemed to be all around me now. And it seemed as though I were damned if I remembered it and damned if I didn't. When I had gone to the psychiatrist, seeking help, he had made matters worse. Now what choice did I have except to return to denial? And even though the truth kept surfacing, I continually tried to suppress it.

So I searched the Internet, went to various job sites and sent out my resume. The fact that I now had some international experience definitely worked in my favor.

In the end, I took the first job that was offered to me. I would be working as a receptionist in a four–star hotel on one of the Greek islands. A telephone interview was all the hotel manager required. Although I didn't speak Greek, he was impressed with my Caribbean experience and my languages skills, particularly since he wanted to accommodate his clients in as many languages as possible.

It sounded like an ideal job opportunity, especially since the island offered so many water sports such as sailing, scuba diving, snorkeling and windsurfing. And then there were the other experiences that I relished like visiting ancient ruins and dining on mouthwatering Greek cuisine.

Before I left home, I sent out applications to various schools. Going through school brochures had kept me occupied since I had returned in November, and then, of course, there had been Christmas with all the shopping and preparations that involved. Also, several stores needed extra staff so it was easy to get a job.

I knew I had to get on with my life, but pretending to be the ambitious, focussed person I had been would be hypocritical. I suppose I just sent out applications as a sort of safety net. You never knew what I might want later on. For the moment, all I wanted was to get away. It had been hard enough to explain away my moods by claiming that I wanted to travel until I could make up my mind which studies I wanted to pursue. Actually, I didn't even know if I wanted to study at all. Part of me wanted my life back so badly, but I felt that it was no longer an option. Too much had happened. I had no choice but to continue on this new path. There was no honest way back.

Auntie Rosalie wasn't particularly happy about me leaving again. She wanted me to have some stability in my life, no matter what it was. I promised her this job was only for the summer season so that, if I wanted to, I could start school when I returned. It was March now. I would still have about six months to reflect.

***

From the hot, stuffy Greek airport, I took a taxi to the hotel, located on the northeastern end of the island in a town called Nyx. The thirty–minute journey allowed me to become acquainted with my new destination. We passed a village, the winding streets of which were lined with balconied white–washed houses and pine trees. There was a fortified tower and Byzantine basilicas, interspersed with bustling, modern towns. We passed harbors and fishing villages, and I even caught sight of an archeological site: the remains of a classical Greek temple with fluted columns, some with the ornamental capitals intact, and a pediment on one side. And then, finally, we came to the Zacharias hotel, named after the original owner, the current owner's grandfather.

It was a marvelous sprawling beach resort. Entering the reception area I was overcome by a sense of serenity. Certainly the ride from the airport had been nerve–wracking due to the crazy afternoon traffic and the risk–taking habits of my driver. But now my heart slowed down as I proceeded to the cool, marble counter in a lobby decorated with bronze sculptures and paintings that depicted events from the Greek mythology.

"From the relieved look on your face I can tell you just had your first Greek road experience," the receptionist, Carola, said with an enormous smile.

Carola was a fair–skinned, blue–eyed, twenty–one–year–old German girl with short blond hair, who had worked in the hotel the previous year, as well. She was so spontaneous and cheerful, a true gem. And I was delighted to meet someone I knew could be a friend.

She called someone to show me to my room, which was on the ground level in the quiet area at the back, with an outside door so I wouldn't have to enter and leave through the hotel lobby. Reception staff was entitled to half–board, and Carola also told me I would get a rental car, the hotel manager having been able to arrange a good deal with a local company due to the large amount of business he brought in from hotel guests but also because he wanted his foreign personnel to be able to explore the island. Carola added that he pampered us to ensure we'd come back each year.

The Zacharias hotel was a white–washed, five–story building situated in a relatively quiet part of the huge sheltered bay that was enclosed by hills. Set on the edge of a pebble beach, the balconies and patios offered splendid views of the beckoning sea or of the hills, which were now carpeted with spring flowers such as white cyclamens, irises, anemones, poppies, lilies, and daisies. The hotel catered to a broad international clientele that mainly consisted of families, couples in their late–twenties and thirties, and elderly people.

I was glad I would be working in a quiet environment. Although it would be busy once the summer season fully set in, it was clear that it would still be far more peaceful than a club hotel with loud music being pumped out day and night.

Although I knew that I needed to work in order to have some distraction from the trauma that occupied my mind, at the same time, I longed for some peace, and I hoped that, since the hotel would be relatively quiet in spring, I would be able to relax a bit, because having had my guard up all the time at home and my constant secretiveness had exhausted me.

I put my things in my spacious room, a place of warmth and tranquility, with cedar furnishings, twin beds, white walls decorated with paintings of colorful fishing boats out at sea, and a large glass door that offered a breathtaking view of the aquamarine sea. After a brief rest, I decided to explore the hotel. Starting at the other side of the corridor, at the pale blue TV room with armchairs clotted with pillows, I passed the dining area, a brightly lit, large room with a buffet in the center and white linen tablecloths that draped over the tables, stopping to take a quick peek at the menu, which featured specialties such as Greek salad with feta cheese, moussaka, pastitio, and baklavas.

Outside, beyond the pool area complete with deckchairs and bulky towels, was the alluring beach. Unable to resist, I took off the slippers I had put on after my nap and felt the cool gray–black pebbles between my toes. Since it was still spring, there were few people about, but I knew that very soon this uncrowded beach would be transformed with water–skis breaking the surf and windsurfers gliding across the waves in the blazing heat of summer.

That same afternoon I met with the hotel manger, Mr. Alexiou, a short, middle–aged, bearded Greek, who briefed me on my responsibilities, which were similar to those I'd had in the Caribbean. He told me that I would be working closely with Carola for the first week, so that she could show me the ropes, and I was happy that I would be trained by someone who had been kind enough to invite me for a drink on my first day.

So, later that evening, Carola and I went for a drink at a local bar where she introduced me to some of the other non–Greeks working in Nyx, many of whom in bars or restaurants, for car rental companies, as tour guides on excursions or in museums, and still others in hotels just as we did. And that's where I met Claudio.

Claudio was a thirty–year–old, brown–eyed, dark–haired Swiss of average height and muscular build with a charming grin that disclosed crooked, coffee–stained teeth. He had lived in Greece for six years and worked for the car rental company that provided Mr. Alexiou with free cars, although Mr. Papadakis, Claudio's boss, didn't give his employees cars. Since Claudio was an Italian–speaking Swiss, we spoke English and I immediately fell in love with his beautiful Oxford accent that he had obviously learned from his British father. Claudio's soft–spoken voice made me think that he was a gentle person. That night he was neatly dressed in brown cotton trousers and a perfectly ironed, white shirt. He looked very attractive.

Carola and I sat down on plastic chairs at a wobbly plastic table — garden–furniture that looked odd inside a bar — with Claudio and two of his colleagues, Stavros and Dimitri. Carola told me that the cheap prices on the menu explained the bar's appearance, and later I found out from Claudio that he was paid very little at his job.

Claudio and I had been chatting for a while before we got up to dance. The music that was playing was eighties pop.

"My heart skipped a beat when you walked in," he told me.

I smiled even though I assumed that it was a line he had used many times before.

A pretty girl dressed in a sexy black skirt and a short colorful top walked in. Everyone greeted her as she entered.

"Who's she?" I asked Claudio.

"That's Stella, one of my flatmates and a colleague," Claudio said. "We live in an apartment a few blocks from here."

"How many girls do you live with?" I asked him, loosening my grip and taking a step back.

"Just one," he said. "The other two are men. But I only have eyes for you."

I knew that was a line, too, but I wanted to believe him. It was a time when I was ready to believe a lot of things I shouldn't have.

***

Everything seemed to have fallen into place. I had great colleagues, and Claudio seemed to be a kind–hearted person. He earned so little that I usually had to pay when we went out. But I believed he was thoughtful by giving me chocolate, although he gave me cheap chocolate I didn't like. I suppose I had been spoilt eating Swiss chocolate, which he actually could have known being Swiss himself. But I explained it away with his financial situation. And my colleagues thought he was so sweet to give me these presents. Claudio said he wanted to marry me and have children. And that was exactly what I wanted to hear. I believed what I wanted or rather needed to believe. Anything to fix the shambles I had made of my life.

Perhaps I should have realized from the start that it would never work. I had always been this bright and extremely motivated overachiever, whereas Claudio had dropped out of high school to spend several years in the army after which they had asked him to leave. I never found out why.

Another drawback was that we had a major communication problem because he had the tendency to become bored with our conversations very quickly, since I liked to talk about books I had read, films I had seen, water sports I had done and about discovering the island together, but he was only interested in kissing me and touching me, which I understood as a display of his love for me, at first. And, although it had initially pleased me that he asked no questions about my past, his total disinterest in my life soon came to be a much bigger problem than I had ever anticipated.

But I suppose not being connected to him was something I had chosen to ignore. Or, at least, tried to ignore. I was so in love with the illusion of having a life that I tended to live in a fantasy. Since I was still very much affected by the trauma of the rape, my decisions were irrational on many levels. Primarily, I was desperately afraid of never being able to have a normal life again. My common sense was gone. I could no longer rely on my judgement or even my instincts. And because Claudio and I were so unconnected it wasn't possible to have a proper conversation.

I actually thought choosing a man who was Swiss would be a sensible thing, believing that I could more readily trust and rely on someone who had the same roots, despite the fact that he had been raised in the Middle East. I suppose I was merely clinging to anything that appeared secure and trustworthy to stop myself from going completely insane.

***

Before I met Claudio, I had considered having a one–night stand, hoping that if I could just enjoy sex once, perhaps I would be cured. I think now that that was a big part of why I decided to sleep with Claudio. Primarily, the fact that he said he loved me and wanted us to marry and have children made it seem like the sort of thing I had dreamed of. I just wanted to believe it all too much. And, I suppose, too, that I rushed into a relationship with him in the hope of experiencing sex in a way that had nothing to do with pain. I wanted this part of my life dealt with. I was fed up with wondering what it could be and should be like. I wanted the Caribbean specter to disappear. I knew I was the only one who could solve this, and by being hesitant I thought I'd never get the job done.

As Claudio was thirty and had previous experience, I figured he'd notice that I was far more nervous than any normal girl and also afraid. So I told him about what had happened to me. And because he didn't react I should have known to leave him right then and there. He was so indifferent. I tried to tell him about what I had suffered and about not having been able to have the criminal put away. But he wasn't moved by it at all. He even seemed sort of annoyed that I had wanted to tell him. He didn't say he was sorry it had happened to me. Ironically, at that moment, when I would have liked him to hold me — simply for comfort, not sexually — he didn't.

We sat on the beach together one evening to talk more about getting married, because I most certainly had reservations.

"I love you," he said, looking at me with desperate eyes.

"Do you love me more now than when you first met me?" I asked him.

Since we had these communication problems I wanted him to give me at least one good reason why he loved me that would prove that he knew something about who I really was.

After apparently giving it some serious thought he replied, "No, I feel the same."

"But you didn't know me at first," I insisted. "Now that you know me, don't you love me more?"

"No," he replied firmly. And then, probably seeing the hurt in my eyes, he added, "Sometimes you just know. My parents got married two weeks after they met."

Perhaps he was right. But it didn't feel right. Still, what did I know? I was so confused. At that point I would have believed anything.

We had sex. At his place. Stella had gone back home to Athens for a week, and his two other flatmates generally stayed out until the early hours. It was not a particularly pleasant experience, but I managed to get through it and it didn't hurt. It didn't last very long either. When he had finished, Claudio went to the bathroom to clean himself up and that was pretty much it. Not wanting to spend the rest of the night there with him, I got dressed and went back to my room at the hotel.

At first I felt that I had accomplished something, taken an initial big step, even though I hadn't enjoyed it. I considered this to be a tiny personal breakthrough. Who would have thought I ever would have considered sex to be that?

Later, I wanted to talk to Claudio more in depth about how difficult it was for me. He had basically ignored me when I had tried telling him that the night we had sex.

"This whole sex thing is still pretty uncomfortable for me," I said to him one evening a few days later in the living room of his apartment. I wanted to tell him how I was feeling. I needed to have him understand.

He sighed, clearly annoyed. "At your age you should be having sex," he snapped. "Just get over it."

"It's really difficult for me, you know," I replied, both astonished and hurt.

"You just have to try harder, make a real effort," he said, raising his voice angrily, obviously upset.

"Well, I feel I've already achieved quite a lot by going all the way with you," I told him. "For me that's a big step."

His response was to get up and go to his room. By the time he came back, one of his flatmates had returned and that pretty much rounded off the conversation, and I made up an excuse to leave. He walked me to the door, clearly expecting a kiss, even though he must have known I didn't want to give him one. But the look in his eyes warned me not to challenge him, and, although I was extremely angry with him for not showing any understanding or concern for my situation, in the end I kissed him, because I wanted to leave immediately and didn't want to embarrass him in front of his flatmate, or worse, let on that I had a problem.

I suppose it was much like the obligatory kiss goodnight that my aunt and uncle had always demanded even when an argument had not been resolved. The forced intimacy then had represented their belief that everything was all right. Tampering with that belief was not an option. And now, with Claudio, I felt an odd sense of familiarity. I felt I had no choice but to submit to the kiss, although it all felt so incredibly wrong. But his psychological pressure was too much for me.

But I hadn't given up yet. The following week we went out for a drink, and he came back to the hotel with me.

"What turns you on?" he asked me, as we lay down on the bed.

I didn't know. How could I? I'd never had proper sex before. "What do you mean?" I asked.

He sighed. "Well, what makes you wet? There."

I tried to explain to him that I didn't know, but clearly that seemed incomprehensible to him.

"I know what I like," he said. "I really like it when someone licks my nipples."

Now I understood why he had done that to me. But it had not been pleasant at all. He hadn't been gentle, and he had been in such a rush.

"Can't we just discover what I like together," I asked, "take our time, do it one step at a time?" But the answer was clear.

"How can you not know what you like?" he asked indignantly, shaking his head and rolling his eyes."

"You know why I don't know," I said. "I've never done this before."

"Then find out what you like!" he yelled, rolling off the bed to get a drink of water.

Naturally, his attitude upset me. I felt so alone. He clearly didn't want to help me. It was very much my problem. One I had to solve on my own.

When he returned to the bed, he put my hands on his hard penis.

"I don't want to," I told him.

"You didn't want to do that last time either," he complained.

"I don't want to," I repeated. "I don't feel comfortable with it."

"You have to try harder," he ordered me, his eyes warning me not to disobey. "You'll enjoy it later on."

I felt guilty and self–conscious, perhaps partly due to the fact that I had no experience, but mainly because I felt so uncomfortable with it all to the extent that it nauseated me. But he was happy, and as long as he was satisfied, he didn't see any problems. He just forced me to do things I wasn't ready for and really didn't want to do. But I submitted in order to keep my dream alive, a dream that was so incredibly important to me that I was willing to suffer with Claudio to secure it.

***

We had been going out for a while, but because Claudio was always touching me when we were in public, despite the fact that I told him over and over again not to, we finally broke up.

It happened after one evening when Carola, her eighteen–year–old brother Thomas, who was visiting for two weeks, Claudio and I were walking back after having attended a performance of Greek folk dance.

"Can't you just let me be for a few minutes?" I said annoyed, pushing his arm away from me.

"Look at all these other couples," he said, as though I were a child. "They're all holding and kissing each other. But you never want to."

I wasn't normal. That was his message. Other couples were all cuddly, so we should be, too. And again, he put his arm around me as though he were entitled to do that, as though it were his right no matter what I said.

Later, Carola said I should break up with him, that he clearly didn't respect my wishes, and that what I was asking was not a tall order. She even tried to talk to him about it. But he just felt sorry for himself. So eventually we did.

After that, he seemed to become completely obsessed with me. He always looked depressed. Not because he loved me, but because he had been dumped and was a victim. But we still met a few times as we had agreed to stay friends.

I had talked to Auntie Rosalie about it on the phone and she had said all men were like that, always wanting to hold you and never understanding anything you said to them.

But I did miss the illusion of having a boyfriend. I desperately wanted to be normal. Maybe I just felt that I had failed. After all, it was my fault. I hadn't wanted him to touch me even though he was my boyfriend. I was the one with the problem, not him — at least that was what I believed then. In fact, I thought I should be grateful to him for putting up with me. After all, he could have dated any other girl who didn't have this problem. Looking back, I see how easy it was for me then to blame myself for everything.

***

A few weeks later Nicholas came over for a three–day visit, and I was thrilled. I suggested he meet Claudio. I suppose I wanted my cousin to meet him as, after all, he was the man I had slept with, although I didn't tell Nicholas that.

As usual the first thing Claudio said was, "Hello gorgeous," even though I had told him I hated to be called that, particularly since he always implied just the opposite, telling me that I was overweight. Certainly he must have known then that I didn't feel gorgeous, and that made what he said sound more like sarcasm than a compliment. But Claudio had said girls loved hearing that, so each time he saw me he'd say it. Meaning it didn't matter, and the fact that I hated it didn't matter. It was supposed to be that way. It seemed that Claudio had certain things drilled in his head that you couldn't possibly get out. Of course, people could tell me that there was no harm in being called gorgeous, but that was not the point. It was just another example of how he ignored my feelings and my needs. I had mentioned this to some of my female colleagues, but they told me there was no harm in it and that they would have liked their boyfriends to call them gorgeous which just led to me blaming myself and putting up with it.

Just as most people I knew, Nicholas liked Claudio. Even though he only met him once for dinner, as he had to go to a business conference in Athens, his conclusion was that Claudio was a nice guy. Since the money from Claudio's last paycheck had already run out, I settled the bill that night, telling Nicholas that, as friends, we took turns in paying for meals, because I was too embarrassed to tell him the truth about the man I had been involved with. I missed my cousin terribly when he had left. At the time, he had no idea about the rape, and I had no intention of telling.

***

I agreed to have one more try at sex. I suppose my determination to see this thing through overpowered my fear.

Claudio and I had only had intercourse twice. The first time I didn't want to touch his genital area: the very sight of his penis reminded me too much of the rape. To me that male body part was a weapon, a weapon that had injured me badly, and as a result, I didn't want to look at it or touch it. Even though I made this clear, the second time we had sex, Claudio put my hands on his penis and said I had to try. I really didn't want to but did for a while just to please him. He continually repeated that at my age I should be able to have sex, that I should try harder and get over the rape. After all, he rationalized, all my friends were having sex, so I should just pull myself together and act my age.

In all honesty, if I hadn't been raped, I wouldn't have slept with him. But once my precious gift had been brutally stolen I felt that I had nothing left. I had been used, so what was the point of saving myself now? If I slept with Claudio again it wouldn't matter. Or maybe I kept on sleeping with him just because I wanted to have a normal sex life so badly.

On a Thursday evening, I met with Claudio at his apartment as we had agreed to stay friends. Although I was afraid and hesitant, I let him kiss me, and we went to his room. Very soon his groin demanded attention. He removed my hands from his neck and pushed them downward on to his genitals.

And then, suddenly, I saw him again, the rapist. That monster had just appeared. I didn't see Claudio's face anymore. It was his now. This criminal had wormed himself into my life so completely that I was genuinely frightened.

I stood back and slowly Claudio's face emerged from this other's. After a few deep breaths I forced myself to have sex with him. In a strange way, I felt that I had to pay for the rape first before I could enjoy sex. Only then would I be free, if that ever happened.

So we were back together. But things were just the way they had been before. One day Claudio and I drove to the other side of the island to see a religious procession in which costumed men and women holding icons walked down the streets singing hymns. Some of Claudio's friends had come along and had booked a hotel in the area. But Claudio and I had arranged to stay with Elena, a local tour guide Carola had introduced me to at a party.

Elena was a strong, vivacious, self–confident, thirty–year–old Greek woman and someone who didn't put up with crap from anyone. I thought she was terrific. Elena later told me that she had seen how Claudio couldn't respect my wishes by constantly touching me again. So it wasn't just in my head.

At a certain point, I was so fed up with his touching me, especially since Claudio knew that was the very reason we had broken up before, that I just took off without saying a word and went to stand with Elena, who had walked on to watch another part of the procession further down the street, only to have Claudio come running after me. Couldn't he leave me alone for a few minutes? After all, it wasn't as though I had left him by himself. His friends were there with him. But no. He had to be beside me, touching me every chance he got.

That evening I lay, fully clothed, on top of the bed that I had to share with Claudio, trying to make it clear that I didn't want him coming anywhere near me.

"Great!" he cried out, poking me in the back. "You're in one of your moods again. Can I at least have a kiss goodnight?"

"I'm really tired, Claudio," I said, not having any intention of facing him. "I want to go to sleep."

"Just one kiss," he said firmly.

"I'm too tired. Goodnight," I had replied, raising my voice. I closed my eyes and tried to pretend that I wasn't hearing his muttering and complaining.

After a while he stopped complaining and let me sleep although I didn't, of course, because I was so angry. And to top it all off, he didn't even seem to understand that there was something wrong.

The next day, we drove back, and I dropped him off at his apartment.

"Can I have a kiss?" he asked me, as if everything were all right between us, although I hadn't said a word to him that morning and the entire journey back.

I just couldn't. While avoiding to look at his face in the same way I had always avoided looking at the needle when I had blood drawn, because I believed that seeing the actual deed would be too painful, I now moved my head toward him, waiting for him to take what he felt was rightfully his. I don't know why I was prepared to let him kiss me. Maybe just not to make a fuss out of it. After the kiss I would leave, and it would be over anyway. I was prepared to pay that small price. God only knows why.

Claudio even crossed the road to wave goodbye as I drove off. To the outside world he was so perfect, so attentive: telling me he loved me, offering me gifts, calling me gorgeous. But deep down inside, I hated him.

For days I avoided him, ignoring his phone calls. I had told him to leave me alone for a while, but apparently he couldn't. But I had decided it was over. I just had one minor technicality to take care of and that was to tell him. I called him to make arrangements to meet. That night he was waiting in a bar, neatly clad in black trousers and a blue shirt. Sitting there he looked like the perfect gentleman. Until he spoke.

"I'm being dumped, aren't I?" was the first thing he said when I sat down opposite him at a table at the back of the bar.

I hated the way he always managed to feel sorry for himself.

"Look, you know why we broke up the last time," I said, trying to be firm. "But you just don't learn. You keep on touching me in public."

"All couples do that," he proclaimed, clearly outraged. "It's just you who has a problem with it."

"Well, you knew what the terms were when we got back together," I said to him. "If you can't live with them, then don't go out with me."

"You never even gave it a decent try," he said accusingly. "The last couple of days I haven't even known if I had a girlfriend. I've talked to my friends. They see how you treat me."

I knew that he had often spoken to many people about our relationship in which he was always the victim and I was treating him so cruelly. If all those people only knew.

The conversation that we had — if you could even call it that — led absolutely nowhere and ended by my telling him that I didn't want to see him for a while. Because Claudio had laid such a guilt trip on me I couldn't bring myself to break up with him permanently then. Somehow he had me in his power, and I was too weak to release myself from his grip. He seemed to have a gift for pushing up my guilt level, although that couldn't have been very difficult because I had felt guilty about practically everything since the attack in the Caribbean. But I made it even easier for him because my mind was such a mess. I couldn't hold any rational thought for very long. I questioned all of my decisions and therefore couldn't stick with them.

Also, I wasn't able to convince myself to stop believing that if I left Claudio I would most certainly abandon my dream of only sleeping with the man I would marry. I was afraid that the next person I became involved with, after leaving Claudio, would not be caring either. How many men would I end up sleeping with then? After all, my aunt and uncle had often said that many couples got divorced because they couldn't fight for a relationship and thought that they would be happier with another person, when in fact they quite often ended up trying over and over again with different partners. Auntie Rosalie had told me over the phone that there were tough times in every relationship and by leaving when things were difficult, I would never be able to make it work with anyone. So, in spite of my brave resolution to call it quits, I was back to square one, to playing it safe and toughing it out with Claudio.

***

On the first and only Sunday I was off, because I had worked extra shifts earlier that week covering for a colleague who had been sick, Claudio and I went diving. I relished the thought of seeing the typical Mediterranean rock walls, underwater caves, rock reefs, fish and sponges that I had discovered on previous dives Carola and I had done with the same diving center. After a short walk, in dry, boiling hot wetsuits, from where the diving instructor had parked the van, Claudio and I headed toward a shallow area to put on our fins, while the other people in our group were briefed on the dive, which, according to the diving instructor, we didn't need since we had both done this dive before. But after I had sat down in the water I had trouble keeping my legs from floating up.

"Are your legs really that weak?" Claudio asked me annoyed. "Push them down!"

"I can't," I told him as I struggled with the heavy yellow tank on my back, feeling extremely embarrassed about my weakness.

"Don't you have any muscles in your legs?" he cried disdainfully, grabbing my right ankle and pulling the blue fin out of my hand, in the process dislodging the other.

"The other one!" I shouted, pointing to the fin that was being carried away by the clear waters. Claudio dropped my right leg and retrieved the other fin.

"My legs really are that weak," I told him, not, incidentally, for the first time. "I've never been good at anything physical."

"That's not true," Claudio said, standing back after he had put on my other fin. "I think you're very good physically, the best." The horny look on his face made me realize he meant sex. Why was that always on his mind?

"I never like sex," I said, pulling myself up on the rocks in this shallow area. "How can you like it so much when you know that I hate it?"

"You'll like it later on," he said sharply, deflecting my remark.

After a few moments of silence he added, in a sulking tone that made me think he felt sorry for himself again, "If these problems continue I'll get a book or something."

I suppose he felt sorry that he might actually have to make the effort of getting that book. Although I should have known he never would, because then, I saw his self–satisfied smile again, the one he'd always worn after he'd had his orgasm, the one that obviously meant that he would serve himself and didn't give a damn about me.

And I should have known that in the same way he had often promised to take me out to a fancy restaurant and treat me but never did, he would not get me a book either. I so much wanted him to take this opportunity to show me that he *did* care. But every time I asked him about it afterward he became upset and said that he hadn't got round to it yet.

I had always been in charge before, but then, when I needed it most, I was not. My life was being lived by someone else.

When the rest of the group arrived, I was surprised that the instructor paired me up with another girl and Claudio with an older man. And I was happy that I could enjoy the dive swimming next to someone with whom I could feel at ease.

However, oddly enough, there was an important task that apparently only Claudio could accomplish.

He and I went for walks quite often: along the shore or past the stores. And, as strange as it may seem, when Claudio was around, the specter wasn't. In fact, since I had become involved with Claudio the specter seemed to appear less and less. Perhaps it *was* working then. Perhaps by being married to Claudio I would be free of him. Then it was just a matter of hanging in there.

***

When I had slept with Claudio, I knew that I could survive sex. I knew that if I wanted to I probably would be able to become pregnant. I had worried about not being able to ever have children because I couldn't endure sex. But now I knew that even though I didn't like it, maybe it was a small price to pay to have children. I mostly thought of what I had learned from that film I had watched with Nicholas: I tried to separate my body from my mind. After all, that's all Claudio wanted: my body. He said we had a great chemistry, but I didn't know what he was talking about.

I had thought of talking to Carola about my problems, but I felt too embarrassed to tell her what was happening, because I was ashamed of my ignorance and inexperience.

I was becoming so desperate that, although I had never intended to do so, I decided to tell Auntie Rosalie that I had been raped when she came to visit me in Nyx, after a short stay in Lausanne, where she had gone to visit my grandmother, who had tripped and fallen down the stairs and broken an arm. Auntie Rosalie wanted to take the strain off Grandpa and had therefore asked for time off work.

I went to pick her up at the airport around ten o'clock in the evening. Luckily I had been able to switch shifts with Carola. Mr. Alexiou had agreed to let Auntie Rosalie sleep with me in my room. She was even entitled to half–board, like me. I was so excited that she was coming, looking forward to introducing her to all the beauties of the island. But more importantly, I needed Auntie Rosalie to help me find a way out of the misery I was in, and I was hoping that by confiding in her I would get my answer. More than anything, I wanted her to tell me that there were valid reasons for leaving Claudio, that I shouldn't have to put up with what he was doing to me. Since I was incapable of relying on my own judgement, I suppose I needed her approval. I needed her say that it was okay to take the easy way out and break up with Claudio for good.

Auntie Rosalie was a slender woman in her forties with shoulder–length brown hair that she always wore neatly tied back from her face. She was a woman who looked after herself, and you could tell. That night she was wearing a long, bright, red, summer dress and carrying a black cardigan that she had probably needed inside the cooler aircraft. She came toward me, pushing a trolley containing her two bags, and took my face in her hands, a gesture that was so intimate that it surprised me and made me cry. Knowing the way she had brought me up, she must have realized that something had to be really wrong if I was showing this much emotion. Right then and there she must have known that I was not all right.

We had a drink at the airport, just to settle me down, and then drove to the hotel. After Auntie Rosalie had freshened up she sat on my bed.

"Come sit down next to me," she said, stroking the flowered print cover.

That was when I told her about the rape. Half way through I couldn't go on. I let my head fall on the bed and sobbed incessantly. Auntie Rosalie just let me cry, gently stroking my hair. She had never been this affectionate before. Clearly she wanted to make it all right, to make it all better. But, of course, she couldn't. I continued my story, sobbing and sniffing, occasionally brushing away my tears. I didn't want to hurt her and, in a way, felt selfish doing so, particularly since I knew that she had been upset about my grandmother, but I really couldn't handle this anymore on my own.

The next day I had to work, and Auntie Rosalie spent her day relaxing at the hotel pool, although I'm sure she must have been deeply troubled by what I had told her.

That evening we had arranged to have dinner with Claudio at a little family–owned restaurant a short walk away from the hotel. Claudio was neatly dressed in trousers and a jacket — he even wore a tie. He was extremely polite and very courteous to Auntie Rosalie. The typical, reserved English gentleman, the act I had initially fallen for. We mainly talked about the places my aunt should visit during her stay, and I was baffled since this was the first time I heard Claudio having a proper conversation, as opposed to him just wanting to touch me and kiss me, and I realized that my aunt would be impressed with all the helpful tips he was providing about exploring the island, based on his own six–year experience here.

The dinner truly felt awkward. Having Auntie Rosalie meet Claudio made it all seem so official, and that made me feel as though I were being backed into a corner. We may have looked happy together, trying to hold up an act, but we weren't, or at least I wasn't.

Auntie Rosalie paid, saying that was the least she could do as she was getting her accommodation free of charge, and, of course, that let Claudio off the hook easily.

After we had said goodbye to Claudio and walked back to the hotel, I wanted to tell her about how awful it was sleeping with him, but never really managed. I knew she disapproved of premarital sex, but since I had told her that Claudio had asked me to marry him I thought I'd take the risk of telling her. I was so desperate then. I felt that I didn't have anything left to save for someone special anyway. It had already been taken away. How could she blame me?

"Auntie Rosalie, it's so hard with Claudio," I said when we were back in my room. "I told him, but he doesn't seem to understand."

Auntie Rosalie came to sit beside me on my bed. "There is no way a man can understand anything like rape," she said, staring blankly into space. After a short pause she continued. "I can tell Claudio is a sweet, caring man. And you will probably never find anyone who loves you as much as he does. You should be happy to have found someone like him."

I couldn't go into detail about my sexual experiences with Claudio. I felt so embarrassed. But it was also difficult because Auntie Rosalie had experienced sex with my uncle, and, knowing how those two related to one another, I did not think that my aunt's context for making sexual decisions or forming opinions was something that I wanted to use as a base. Since my aunt always gave in to Uncle Stephen and was the one who made sacrifices, I imagined that she would find it difficult to understand a situation in which women did not willingly give in to whatever their partner wanted in the way of sexual favors.

Perhaps Claudio's soft–spoken ways and introverted personality created the illusion to those who were acquainted with him that he was a kind–hearted, gentle person, someone who couldn't possibly be unreasonable or demanding. But, of course, I had seen him in quite a different context, as someone who, when I had confided in him, had simply told me to forget about the rape experience. And as a result, I had not been able to deal with it as I should have. According to him, I shouldn't deal with it at all. I should just be over it.

"You should accept the fact that you cannot expect a man to understand what you have been through," she said, and, to me, it sounded as though she were preaching. "Men are fundamentally different from women, and the sooner you accept that the better. I think you might be expecting too much from Claudio."

I couldn't believe this. Perhaps, if I could bring myself to tell her what was going on, she might understand that it all felt so wrong and horrible. I had learned in school that sex was supposed to be beautiful and something you could both enjoy. Now I realized that in my sex life there was only one of us who found it pleasurable. And it most certainly wasn't me. In fact, I found it revolting.

"I think it did us both good when you went to the restroom, so that Claudio and I could talk," Auntie Rosalie continued, ironing out the creases in her white linen skirt with her hand. "You know he doesn't have anyone to talk to about this. It must be hard for him, too, having to deal with this."

I was baffled, particularly since, at that point, I really didn't believe he cared.

But what I had just heard made me feel even guiltier. I already felt that it was my fault because I lacked sexual experience and didn't know what was supposed to happen or what was expected of me. I was the one with the problem, not him. He was happy, always very satisfied, and he assured me he had the best orgasms, while I begrudged him each one. I hated sleeping with him. But I just kept forcing myself to because I wanted to get this problem out of the way for good. Claudio kept assuring me that I would enjoy sex after a while. And as Auntie Rosalie approved of him, I was led to believe that eventually things would work out. I thought I should trust him and believed that I felt insecure and scared because of the rape. I couldn't follow my own judgement so I relied on Auntie Rosalie's.

The day my aunt flew home, I asked Claudio to come over since I didn't want to be alone. I was so sad that my aunt had left and needed distraction, even if he provided it.

That night, while we were having sex, Claudio actually noticed that I didn't want to. "Thank God," I thought. "Now he's finally going to ask what's wrong and help me." But instead, he became angry. He got up and went to the bathroom.

"I guess I'm just going to have to do it myself then," he yelled out in an accusing tone.

For some reason, probably associated with pride and guilt, I called him back. The thought of not being able to satisfy him seemed so wrong. The idea of him masturbating in my bathroom seemed worse than him using my body. And so I just let him do his thing. When he was finished, he acted as though nothing had to be said about what had happened. Clearly, he felt no responsibility for any of it. I may even have apologized for my behavior, not being able to fulfil his needs.

I wish I had been stronger then. Afterward, after we had split up for good, I had many nightmares about him being on top of me pleasing himself with my body. It made me so sick. It drove me absolutely insane. How on earth could I have let him do that to me? What had possessed me to think I would feel less guilty if he used my body instead of masturbating in my bathroom?

**

Auntie Rosalie left on Friday, and that Sunday afternoon something extremely frightening happened.

Claudio was free on Sundays, but I — except for the time that he and I had gone diving — always had to work. That Sunday, because my first shift had ended at two and I would have to start work again at four, I went to my room to take a shower and freshen up.

After my shower, I walked out of the bathroom in a towel, taking my cosmetic box with me since the bathroom mirror was fogged up and I needed a clear reflection. I went to stand in front of the mirror near the glass door of my room. The door was covered by a thin white curtain, but if you stood right next to it you could see what was going on outside.

As I was spreading my moisturizer out over my face I suddenly heard a loud banging on my glass door. There was a man outside, apparently very upset about something because he banged very hard, several times.

Afraid he would see me, I rushed to the bathroom where I closed the door and waited for the banging to stop. When it finally did, I came out of the bathroom and quickly got dressed, wondering who was trying to come into my room that badly. I thought the man might have broken the glass from the way he was banging on it. What would have happened if he had come in and found me wearing only a towel? The thought of it terrified me.

Then, suddenly, he was back, and the banging started again. I approached the curtain carefully and saw that it was Claudio. Why was he doing that? He was acting like a madman. I saw him put his hands on the glass trying to look in. I was standing so close to the door and was afraid he would see me. For a few moments he leaned his back against my door, fluttering his arms in the air, growling. From his reaction I realized he couldn't see me. I was extremely relieved.

He was now shouting things like, "Where are you?" It was clear that he was very angry. I didn't see why. I had told him I had to work. He knew my day off was Wednesday, not Sunday. What gave him the right to act as though he owned me, as though I had to obey his each and every wish? I felt that I didn't know this man, so I didn't open the door when I recognized him.

After he had spent quite some time peering in, banging and yelling, he took out a piece of paper and a pen, scribbled something down, and then put the note under a rock and placed it in front of my door.

It took quite a while to pull myself back together again. I lay down until it was time to go back to work, unable to decide whether to turn up for my shift or not. What if Claudio was waiting for me? I doubted it since he had left a message. But I didn't want to go see what the note said. When I finally made up my mind to go to work anyway, I left through the inside door of my room.

Working did not take my mind off the incident. I couldn't believe it: my own boyfriend. Now not only did I associate Claudio with my rapist whenever we had sex — something I took full blame for — but even an incident such as his banging on my door was enough to make me associate the two men in my mind. And so the specter had not really gone away. He had merely attached himself to Claudio, and was there, haunting me still.

When I came back after work, I went in through the inside door again. I still didn't want to go look outside to see what the note said. I ate something, watched a Greek song contest on the television and went to bed. To my surprise, I did manage to get some sleep.

The next morning I checked my cell phone. Claudio had sent me a text message saying that he had been by but I hadn't been in. I found that I was surprised that the message had no echo of the anger I had imagined when he had pounded on the door. Perhaps I had been wrong.

The tone of his message gave me the courage to go outside to get the note. Once outside, the first thing I did was peer through the glass door, and I was relieved to find that it was impossible to see anything, even distinct figures or shapes, inside. There was no way he could have seen me. The note was still under the rock. I picked it up and read, "I was here but you weren't. Call me! — Claudio XXX." I tore it up.

When I turned around to walk back into my room, I noticed something hanging on my doorknob. It was a cap marked with the logo of the company Claudio worked for. I had once said to him jokingly that I wanted one of those. Now it irritated me that he could appear to be so thoughtful in small ways and so uncaring about things that really mattered. I didn't want this cap. I just left it hanging there, hoping someone would take it.

I talked to Carola about what had happened, but she couldn't give much advice although she did say that Claudio obsessed over me too much, way too much.

When Claudio confronted Carola about me not being in my room when I had time off between shifts, she tried to make it clear to him that there could always be some kind of emergency that I had to take care of, or a meeting that I had to attend, not to mention the fact that I was free to do what I wanted in my free time. I did not just have to go to my room and wait for him.

The following afternoon, at the same time as I was leaving the hotel on my way to get some office supplies, Claudio arrived in a rental car that he was dropping off for one of the hotel guests. As soon as he saw me, he came running.

Afraid that he would be angry, I immediately told him that I hadn't called him because I had only received his message that morning since I hadn't used my outside door.

"You're always working. We can never spend time together," he said accusingly.

"You know I'm free on Wednesdays," I explained.

"But I have to work then," he said annoyed, raising his arms, palms upward, so as to emphasize how obvious his point was.

When I explained that I had the same problem on Sundays he just looked at me in a spiteful way.

"You often have some time off between shifts on Sundays," he blurted out, pointing his finger at me accusingly.

"I have to work on Sundays, and if I have time off between shifts it is not to spend with you, and you shouldn't take it for granted that I have time off every Sunday because it's clearly not the case," I told him, hoping that he would settle down.

"You work much more than your colleagues," he complained.

Of course that wasn't true. But I didn't want to discuss it then and there. I noticed an elderly couple in the parking lot who had obviously heard Claudio shouting. They averted their glances when they apparently realized I saw them and continued on their way toward the exit. The parking lot was large but luckily almost empty, at least as far as I could tell.

"You know that's utter crap," I said, opening my car door and getting in. "I have to go."

He put his hand on the door so as to prevent me from driving off. "Did you get the cap?" he asked me in an interrogating tone.

"Yes," I snapped.

That was just another example of how he infuriated me by giving me gifts such as chocolate I didn't like, but making an effort to do something that could make me happy, something of importance, that just never happened. It was clear that he had no intention of ever making any sacrifices for me.

Feeling frustrated but also afraid that he would try to stop me again, I quickly pulled the door closed and drove off.

That evening, I did take the cap inside and stashed it way back in my closet so I would not have to see it any time soon. I never wore it and later gave it away to a charity organization.

However, I had been frightened by Claudio's banging on my door, but after a while, I convinced myself that he was not a violent person and that I had been so upset because even that display of anger on his part had triggered my memory of the rape. It had nothing to do with Claudio. At the same time, I wondered why I was always finding excuses for his behavior and blaming myself? I had never been like that before.

***

A month after Auntie Rosalie had left, my high school friend Matt came over for a short holiday. Tall and blond, Matt was an extremely intelligent young man who I had known very well in high school and who was traveling through Europe for the summer months. When he decided to come over to visit me for a few days, I was able to arrange a good deal for his room. Unfortunately, I wasn't able to pick him up at the airport since Carola and I both had to work and there was no one with whom I could switch shifts. As a result, he shared a taxi with some other tourists.

"I'll take the best room you've got," I heard him say in a voice imitating a much older man.

Looking up from where I was working at the reception counter, I was greeted with a wide grin followed by an infectious laugh. "You're here!" I shouted, feeling my face light up. Leaning as far over the counter as I could, I flung my arms around him.

An elderly lady cleared her throat to announce her presence.

"Let me just give him the key," I said to her, trying to remain professional. "I'll be right with you. Here you go, Matt. Room 114. First floor. Take the stairs just around the corner here. My shift is over in half an hour, and then I'm done for the rest of the evening."

"I'll get settled in then," he said. "Come get me when you're ready." Both of us were wearing wide smiles of excitement.

After my shift, I got changed and went to Matt's room. I couldn't believe that he was actually here. Being away from home had been an adventure, but much more so, it had been an escape, and I had missed my friends. When I knocked on the door, he opened it and just stood there, grinning.

"Since you're not going to let me in, would you like to come out?" I said, laughing. "Let's go have a refreshing drink. I know just the place."

Twenty minutes later, we were inching our way through the bustling town, stopping at several jewelry shops to admire the superb craftsmanship and the classical, Byzantine designs, until we came to the narrow dirt road that led to a taverna that was only accessible on foot. The climb was strenuous but rewarding.

We reached the top and sat down at the last available outdoor table on the terrace, both a little exhausted, and watched the sun slowly sink into the sea, but neither the legendary blue, crystalline waters of the sea, nor the alluring beaches could heal me.

Matt must have noticed the distracted, glazed look on my face.

"Are you all right?" he asked.

I nodded.

"It's probably all that hard work, listening to whining tourists, always dealing with complaints," Matt guessed. "Well, forget about them tonight. I promise, I won't complain."

Compared to Claudio those tourists were a breeze. But I wasn't going to get into that with Matt. I didn't want to ruin his stay. So I decided to do as he said: forget about it for tonight. Or, at least, give it a genuine shot.

"Tell me about your travels," I said, keen to find out what he'd been up to. "I'm so excited to hear about what you've done and seen."

In high school Matt had always been filled with energy, integrating quickly with new groups of people. Polite and thoughtful, he was also popular.

He chatted away enthusiastically until we were interrupted by the waitress who came to take our order. It was busy, and she apologized for making us wait. To our enormous surprise, she returned almost immediately with our ice–cold lemonades so that we could quench our thirst.

"Enough about me," Matt said, putting down his half finished drink on the table. "What's going on with you? In your e–mails you mentioned that you had a boyfriend. Can I meet him? I'm curious, you know."

Hearing the excitement in Matt's voice, I agreed.

"Things aren't going that well right now," I told him, "but I'd like you to meet Claudio. That way you can tell me what you think of him."

"All right," Matt said. His eyes searched mine as though he were looking for some kind of explanation.

"I'm okay," I said, breaking the awkward silence. "Don't worry. I'm just tired."

I couldn't tell Matt about the rape or the problems I had with Claudio. Although we had been very close in school and still were, this was way too humiliating. And I couldn't let it spoil Matt's stay, although it was hard to conceal my pain and loneliness.

At my request, Matt continued his stories about his travels, and I was able to put on a happy act for the remainder of the evening and was pretty convinced that he bought into my performance. We talked about old times, but all those memories seemed to be from a different lifetime. One I now felt banned from.

After a leisurely stroll back to the hotel, we both retired to our rooms. I was glad Matt was here but, at the same time, he reminded me of the carefree girl I could never be again.

***

I had made it very clear to Claudio that Matt could not drink alcohol because he used to have a drinking problem brought on by family difficulties. I mentioned it to Claudio twice to make sure he understood and wouldn't forget.

The following night, Matt, Claudio, Carola and I went out to a quiet local bar. I had told Carola that I couldn't possibly take Matt to the bar with the plastic furniture, because I would be too embarrassed. Around eight o'clock we all left the hotel together and made our way along the narrow, winding streets and out to the waterfront bars. Carola and I led the way, giggling about a complaint we'd received from a female guest who had said that there was too much choice on the buffet and that it was such a strenuous task deciding what to eat every morning. The guys followed us.

We sat down at a table on the terrace. The view of the glistening blue sea and the traditional Greek music that was playing softly in the background made for a typical holiday setting. Matt and Carola sat on one side of the table and

Claudio and I sat on the other. She and I were chatting when Matt and Claudio got up.

"We're going to get the drinks. What do you want?" Matt asked, trying to get past Carola.

She pulled her chair closer to the table, making it easier for him to get through. "Mineral water for me," I said.

"I'll have mineral water, too, thanks," Carola told Matt.

"All these people on holiday and we're working," I said, feeling a bit envious of the holiday–makers, as I frequently did since, although I liked my job a lot, we had long shifts. Luckily they were never nightshifts, however. The latest I'd ever had to work here was until eleven.

"Yes, but they have to leave sooner," Carola remarked with a grin on her face.

We both started laughing.

"Are you two still giggling?" I heard Matt ask as he put down our drinks on the table. "We're just going to play darts in the back. All right?"

"Have fun," I said, patting him on the shoulder, "and try to win."

"I'll do my best," Matt replied, laughing.

I wondered if Claudio had recently received his salary and therefore had not run out of money yet — something he blamed on his poor budgeting skills — or if Matt had paid. I knew Matt would most certainly have offered to pay and I also knew that Claudio would have had no problem indulging in his generosity.

Carola and I spent most of the evening just relaxing, trying to blend in with the surrounding tourists, who clearly deserved a long needed break away from it all.

Around twelve o'clock, we were starting to doze off so I went inside to get Matt and Claudio. During the walk back to the hotel, Carola and I were too tired to pay much attention to the intriguing dart stories Matt and Claudio had to tell.

I assumed all had gone well until the next day when I heard otherwise from my friend.

Matt and I had agreed to meet in my room after my shift at four o'clock. I had changed out of my uniform and into a comfortable short sleeve white shirt and turquoise skirt when, hearing a firm knock on the door, I opened it and saw a smiling, slightly sunburned Matt.

"Didn't use any sunscreen, did you?" I teased him, letting him in.

"I did actually, but I fell asleep on the beach," Matt replied, closing the door behind him. "But it doesn't hurt, so I'm really glad about that," he added, seating himself on my bed.

"What did you think of last night?" I asked, folding my arms and awaiting Matt's verdict.

"I thought it was pleasant," he said. "Claudio and I got along."

"What happened when you ordered the drinks?" I asked Matt, being my usual curious self.

"Claudio asked me if I wanted a drink," Matt sighed, "but I was firm about having a lemonade. But then Claudio insisted that I have a real drink. He said he didn't want to drink alone, as though it were a macho thing."

I knew I could always count on honesty with Matt, and I was grateful, but hearing this infuriated me and I wanted to confront Claudio. He had tried to hurt my friend in such a cruel way. One drop of alcohol could start him drinking again.

"I told him about the fact that you can't drink," I said. "I told him not to offer you anything."

Matt got up from the bed. "Stop protecting me all the time," he said calmly, placing his hands on my shoulders. "I know you care and mean well, but I can look after myself."

I still felt helpless and guilty about what had happened. I had tried to protect Matt, but hadn't been able to. Luckily he had been strong enough to resist.

"Come on," he said, pinching my cheek. "Let's not worry about it now. I'm going to treat you to some delicious ice–cream, and then we can go to that outdoor museum you were so excited about showing me."

"All right," I said, making a real effort to let it go for now, for Matt's sake, especially since he was leaving the next day. And we were off.

But I did confront Claudio. The next afternoon, after Matt had left, I ran into him as he was walking back to the exit of the hotel after having picked up some papers. I was on my way to give a message to one of the guests who was lying by the pool.

"How could you have done that?" I asked him, my jaw tight with tension, trying to keep my voice down. "I told you he couldn't have alcohol and you even insisted."

He shrugged his shoulders, looking at me as though I were accusing him without a reason.

"Don't you understand how important this was?" I continued, relieved that there were no guests walking past. "Why do you think I told you twice?"

But Claudio just shook his head dismissively, as though it were no big deal.

"Did you just forget?" I asked him, but he turned on his heel and left, reacting as indifferently as he had when I told him about the rape and the fact that sex was difficult for me. The fact was that he didn't care about what I said. There was clearly no point in trying to tell him anything. He made me so angry. This time he had let me down badly. I could deal with him treating me badly — I thought — but when he hurt my friend that was a different matter all together. I was determined to ensure that something like this would never happen again. But my friend had been able to fend for himself. In fact, it was me, who couldn't.

***

In her e–mails, my aunt kept urging me to marry Claudio, saying that he was a wonderful boy. I admit that to the outside world it looked like he adored me. But no one knew of his indifference in bed. And I tried to hold up the act, believing in the illusion that I did have a normal life, that being married to Claudio would make the rape undone. But inside I was dying.

And as the summer wore on I became increasingly depressed. I had begun hyperventilating again. In fact, sometimes I felt as though I were suffocating. I was so miserable and yet so determined. I truly believed that I just had to get through this rough period and once it was over everything would be fine.

But, later on in our relationship, Claudio had insisted we not use a condom anymore, as he felt less sensation with it on. I really didn't want to have unprotected sex and told him so. But he insisted. He had made this decision when he was already on top of me and entered my body as I was telling him I didn't want him to. I had tried to push his body off me, in vain. When he was finished, he said we would be married and have children soon. And since I was taking the pill, at the time, I would not become pregnant anyway.

Afterward, he let it slip, in a careless moment, that he had come inside me without protection before. Apparently one time we were having sex and he had put on a condom as

I had insisted, but feeling no sensation, he had just removed it without me noticing.

I knew I didn't have HIV, because I had been tested after the rape. He said he had been tested, too, but even then I had my doubts. I was tested soon after. However, Claudio refused to be tested again. And he continued to insist that we have unprotected sex, not taking no for an answer.

But I had serious doubts about his being free of disease because of his promiscuous behavior. I knew he had been with someone else during the time we had split up, since he told me he had needed female attention and I wasn't there. I'd found out about it straight away from Carola and had been hurt by it because it had made me feel that our relationship had not been that special to him. He always looked like he was obsessed with me and truly missed me, but I guess I was easily replaced.

But when we got back together I suppose I forgave him, or at least I blamed myself more, as I was the one who had wanted out of the relationship and had rejected him. I convinced myself that it didn't really matter because we had broken up. But he had told me he had used a condom when he had been with the other girl, and at the time I had believed him. Now I wasn't sure.

But even earlier on in our relationship there had been the incident at the small beach house that Carola and her recent German tour guide boyfriend had rented for a week in order to get way from the hotel scene. As usual, Claudio wanted to have sex.

Carola and her boyfriend were having sex in the other room. The walls of the beach house were very thin, and we could hear them making love. In a way, that seemed to make it all right for us. At least, that's the argument Claudio used. If they were doing it, why shouldn't we? I thought that was ridiculous, but also this time my guilt got the better of me.

Claudio was very good at pushing my guilt level up by telling me to stop using the rape as an excuse not to have sex, saying that I should pull myself together and act my age, instead of being selfish and denying him sex because I insisted on complaining like a baby.

Claudio only told me at the last minute that he hadn't brought a condom. I was still telling him I didn't want him entering me without a condom when he did, not taking any notice of what I said. He said he'd pull himself out before ejaculating.

He always came very quickly. It seemed to be less than a minute that he was inside me. Then he pulled himself out and came all over me. It was so disgusting. His sperm was pouring out over my body. It ran over my legs and on to the sheets. I tried to wipe it off my body with the sheets, but it was sticky and gooey. My pubic hair was covered in it. He might as well have urinated on me.

I convinced myself that, as he hadn't ejaculated inside of me, it was okay: I wouldn't catch any diseases. It had all happened so quickly. But I didn't feel comfortable at all. Still, as it had already happened, what could I do except try to get some peace of mind somehow? I even asked him if he was sure he hadn't got anything inside me. Of course, he said he hadn't. As if he could have known. But I knew this way of having sex was still not safe. Any fluid or sperm released inside prematurely could cause diseases and pregnancy. Only, I couldn't bring myself to think about it then since the damage had already been done. Just as I had done after the rape, I told myself to hang in there and deny it for six months until I was sure I was not infected.

Ashamed to think what Carola would think when she saw sperm all over the sheets — although I don't think the thought of it even occurred to Claudio, let alone embarrassed him — I rolled them up the next morning, hoping she would decide to wash them. I asked her if she wanted me to wash them, but she said she would do it. I never knew if Carola noticed the sperm or not because she never mentioned it.

The next time we were together, Claudio just assumed I would let him do the same thing, but I told him to get a condom. He didn't have one. I asked him what he had done with other girls. He said they always took care of it. But the reason I hadn't bought any condoms was out of pure principle. The pill I took was already quite expensive, so I thought the least he could do was buy the condoms. I thought I had made that perfectly clear to him. He had agreed to it. This time sticking to my principles had perhaps not been such a smart move.

Finally, he went to the bedroom his flatmate was using and got one from him. For once then he did respect my wishes, although that might have been the time he took it off without my noticing.

These might have seemed like small things to some, and I know they were to him, but to me his thoughtlessness in regard to sex had begun to assume enormous importance. Sometimes it seemed to me that everything that had anything to do with this sort of intimacy had been tainted for me forever.

***

One evening, about a week after Matt had left, Carola and I watched a film in the hotel TV room. We were both off that evening and just wanted to relax. The TV room was usually quiet and also this evening the film had not attracted many viewers. Only an elderly British couple and a younger Austrian couple, who I guessed to be in their late twenties, had made it that night. We all sat in comfortable armchairs, clustered around the screen. It was actually quite cozy and homey, with feet dangling from the sides of the armchairs and heads resting on the armrests. Off work was off work. And no uniform certainly meant off work.

It was wonderful. The film was relaxing and funny, and, since it didn't require much concentration, my mind wandered off. I couldn't remember when I had last been in an environment that had made me feel so at ease, so secure, so safe. No one in this room was pressuring me to do anything, let alone things that I really didn't want to do. I had forgotten that this was possible. Life didn't have to be so full of tension. And I realized just how badly I wanted to run away from Claudio. I couldn't deal with it anymore. I just wanted out.

***

Later on I got a vaginal infection and having sex genuinely hurt. Claudio said it wasn't normal that I felt any pain and just continued to take what he felt was his privilege. Nothing was more important to him than his orgasm, and everything that got in the way had to be dealt with firmly. I repeatedly tried closing my legs and pushing him away, telling him it really hurt, but he just pushed my legs open again and grabbed my wrists, holding them down next to me on the bed so he could do what he wanted. Crying, begging or struggling never made any difference. He would just continue.

I felt trapped. This could not be normal, no matter what my aunt said. Even though I repeatedly told Claudio it hurt, even afterward, he would say, "A little pain never harmed anyone." He told me it was something I should just deal with. I shouldn't whine. It was a small price to pay for (his) pleasure.

Although I didn't understand why I kept going back to him for more, I did realize that it had gone much too far.

In fact, by the end of that week, Mr. Alexiou passed by the reception, saying that he wanted to see me in his office after my morning shift. I wondered if he wanted to see me because I had been very quiet that past week and had been walking around the hotel looking extremely sad, which was a consequence of Claudio's forcing himself on me when I truly was in physical pain. I hoped it hadn't cost me my job.

"I'm afraid I have some very disturbing news for you, Elize, and I hope you won't resent me interfering in your private affairs," Mr. Alexiou began.

Was he going to fire me? Did he mean that I was letting my personal life get in the way of my work?

"I'm sorry that I have to tell you this, but you should know. Yesterday I had dinner with Mr. Papadakis, you know, from the car rental company that gave us your car, incidentally, also, your partner's boss. Well, he asked me if your relationship with Claudio was serious. When I told him it was, he showed me an official letter stating that a particular sum of Claudio's wages is to be deducted each month to pay alimony to his ex–wife for his son."

I was speechless, although now I understood why he was paid so little at his job.

"I'm sorry," Mr. Alexiou said, "but I felt that you had to be told."

"Thank you for letting me know," I finally said, my eyes filled with tears.

The whole relationship was a lie. Had I merely created a world inside my head so that I could hang on to my illusion, the illusion that being married was the only way that I could still have part of my dream, no matter how bad a part I got? However, if it were only an illusion, I now had a reason to get out.

"I can't stay here any longer, Mr. Alexiou," I said, sobbing.

"Then you should leave," he said.

So I quit my job and booked a ticket to nearby Switzerland to go spend some time with my grandparents. One of the reasons I didn't want to go back to the States to see Auntie Rosalie was because she liked Claudio so much and I knew she couldn't handle me blaming him for anything, which is why I decided never to tell her about what Mr. Alexiou had told me. I could not take the risk of Auntie Rosalie explaining Claudio's dishonesty away and pushing me back to him.

I called my grandmother from the airport in Geneva. I hadn't called her from Greece because I didn't want to take the risk of her talking me into staying, and I certainly couldn't tell her why I had to leave over the phone.

She obviously noticed the number I was calling from and became suspicious.

"Are you in Geneva, Elize?" she asked in a soft, yet firm motherly tone.

I began to cry bitterly. "Please let me stay with you and Grandpa for a while?" I begged. "I don't know where else to go."

"Does your aunt know you're here?" she asked me, clearly confused.

"Please don't tell her," I sobbed. "She doesn't understand."

"I can't come pick you up now because your grandfather's out with the car, sweetie. Can you manage by train and bus?" Grandma asked in a very concerned voice.

"Yes, I can manage," I told her. "Please just let me stay with you."

"Of course you can stay here," she assured me. "But are you sick? Do I need to call a doctor?"

"No, that's not necessary," I said, beginning to calm down a little now that I knew that I would be safe with people who loved me.

"We'll talk," Grandma told me. "But then we will have to call your aunt, even if only to tell her you're all right."

I agreed but then realized that I couldn't tell my grandmother about Claudio's dishonesty either, let alone his sexual behavior. I knew she would then discuss this with my aunt, and I certainly couldn't handle both of them telling me to go back to Greece. So I decided not to mention Claudio to her. I was convinced that, once I had told her about the rape, she wouldn't suspect that there was anything else I was hiding from her.

***

I thought that I had started facing the fact that I had been raped and that telling my grandmother might repair the damage that had been done to our relationship when I had stayed with her and my grandfather the previous year. I had felt too ashamed to tell her about the assault and had been afraid that if I told her she would not want to be my grandmother anymore. I feared her judgement. If there was any chance she would blame me for it, I knew I couldn't handle it.

However, I looked at my grandmother through different eyes now. I had always looked up to her and wanted to be just like her. Her opinions were so important to me. And she had many more life experiences. That was still the case, but I had aged drastically since the attack. Instead of looking up to her and wanting to be exactly like her, I now wanted to be who I was before the rape. I wanted to be me, the me I was before.

Arriving at their Lausanne home around five o'clock that afternoon, I was greeted with a tight embrace. Short and thin, my grandmother wore a flowered print dress and silver–rimmed glasses. After a two–minute cuddle, she grabbed the bag I had used as my carry on item on the plane and took it inside. I pulled the other two bags in with me and was told to sit down in the living room while she made some of the herbal tea she adored.

Relieved as I was to be out of Greece, I was reluctant to have an intimate talk with her. But under the circumstances, I knew it could not be avoided.

I sat down in their black leather sofa. Everything seemed different, even the marble mantelpiece littered with antique–looking ornaments and bronze sculptures that I had not seen before. It gave the room an unfamiliar feel. There was no warmth or familiar coziness here. And did it matter? Once we had talked, once I had told her the truth, everything would be transformed into coldness anyway.

The water must have been ready because very soon my grandmother entered with the tea, seating herself opposite me in an armchair.

"So, sweetie, what's the matter?" she asked in a tone that demanded an honest reply.

I twisted my fingers together nervously. "The reason I wanted to come here…" I began hesitantly.

"Yes, what is that?" she asked insistently. "It must be pretty important for you to quit your job, again, and come here."

"Well, I was raped," I said. "It happened when I was working in the Caribbean. I thought you should know."

An awkward silence hung over us. I felt as estranged from her now as I did from the room we were in. There was a connection missing. One that had once been there, but now wasn't.

"Were you ashamed, Elize?" Grandma asked. "Is that why you didn't tell me last year?"

I nodded. I felt blocked inside. I couldn't speak. I couldn't cry. The only thing I could do was just sit there, trying to pretend that I hadn't dropped the bombshell. How could I have been such a fool to hope that once I'd told her about the rape, she might hug me and tell me that everything would be all right? But hope was what I had been living on for so long now. False hope.

However, holding on to that false hope had always seemed better than giving up on marrying Claudio and being reduced to someone my family disapproved of, a person who had multiple sex partners. But more importantly, that was something I had never wanted for myself, although I knew that it had already happened, that Friday, in St. Catherine's. And I wondered if my grandmother was ashamed of me. It was certainly clear that she didn't want to talk about the subject. Instead she asked me about Greece.

After about fifteen minutes, I heard a car stopping.

"Don't tell Grandpa what I told you," I begged her. "It would just upset him."

"I know it would," she said softly. "I won't tell."

I sighed with relief as she left the room.

"Laurent," I heard her say when he came into the kitchen. "Elize's season at the Greek hotel finished early. She'll be visiting us for a while."

"That's terrific," I heard Grandpa say slowly in his deep voice. "When will she be here?"

I gulped.

"Actually, she's just arrived," Grandma told him. "She's in the living room."

Wearing his familiar blue jacket, he came toward me, a balding, slightly hunched, old man who opened his arms to me.

119

"Come give me a hug!" he shouted hoarsely.

I got up and hugged him. But looking over his shoulder I encountered Grandma's disapproving glance. And that's all that was ever said about that.

***

I called Auntie Rosalie that same evening and, just as I could have predicted, she was furious with me for what I had done. She told me to get in touch with Claudio. She said I should get together with him, get to know his family, think about marriage. She, too, believed in only sleeping with one man in your life, and I had already picked mine. If I hadn't been sure, I guess I should have waited. I knew that's how she saw it.

I thought back to a conversation I had once had with Claudio.

"What kind of job will you get when we're married?" I'd asked him one cool evening on the terrace of a quiet taverna overlooking the bay. I had brought him to a place where we could talk because I needed to know how he would support us on his outrageously low income, especially if I became pregnant.

"You're the smart one. You should work," he'd said adamantly, putting his glass of beer back on the table. "I'll stay home with the kids."

I was troubled by his attitude. I didn't want that. "But what if I have a difficult pregnancy?" I had argued.

"Look, we'll be all right," he said, putting his hand over mine. "We'll make sure our children have everything, even if this means we have to go without."

My mouth fell open. How could he talk like this?

"I love you," he added, leaning forward and kissing my cheek. "You're the only one for me. I knew the moment I laid eyes on you that I wanted to spend the rest of my life with you."

And there he went again, uttering such beautiful words that made him seem so committed to our relationship. But the sad truth was, he never meant any of them, and I wasn't strong enough to pay more attention to his actions instead.

"Why don't you take some computer courses so that you can get a better job?" I asked him, since I didn't want to go hungry because he refused to work.

He was clearly not thrilled with my suggestion because he didn't reply. Instead he just took another sip of his beer.

After a few minutes of awkward silence, he added, "You're good at your job. You should work. I can just stay home with the children. We'll save money that way."

But I wanted to stay home with the children. I may have been bright, but I wanted to be the one to raise my babies. I didn't mind working to contribute, but I felt that he should at least make an effort.

I had waited for him to finish his second beer and then called the waitress for the check.

Again, Claudio's pathetic gaze indicated he could not pay for his beers. I should have just paid for my mineral water and let him do the washing up to pay for his drinks. But I just wanted to leave and not deal with it anymore.

"You can't even pay for your own drinks," I said to him softly as we left, shaking my head with disapproval, mainly of myself for having paid for him once again.

"I'll take you somewhere posh, soon," he said. "I promise."

But then he had said that every time I'd had to pay for him. "When?" I asked him, raising my eyebrows, waiting for an answer.

He just shrugged his shoulders and grunted. Did he think I still believed him? But in spite of all that I didn't have the strength to leave him then. In vain, I hung on to the relationship with Claudio for as long as possible, as though I were clasping a thread that could only hold me until it was too thin and broke. And now, it had broken, and I had fallen. As a result, I had been released from Claudio, but I didn't know where I had landed, nor did I know what to do next.

But getting on that plane out of the Greek island had been such a relief. Although I had not admitted it to myself or anyone else then, deep inside I must have realized that I couldn't marry Claudio or have his children. I deserved much better and so did my children. After all, how could I marry someone who had been so completely dishonest with me?

But now I wondered why he wanted children with me if he already had a son. Perhaps his ex–wife didn't let Claudio see him, which I wouldn't blame her for if he had treated her badly, too. And it made sense to me that he didn't want to have another job or have a job at all, since his money would go to his ex–wife anyway, which explained why I had to work to support us both and any children.

But, finally, in Lausanne I was strong enough to admit to myself that I did not want Claudio to be the last person I would ever sleep with. I was still hopeful. I still had faith that there had to be something better out there than this. And even if there weren't, I would not settle for this. I couldn't. All the time in Nyx it had been killing me inside. I'd been wasting away because of it. I had needed to get out and fast. I couldn't possibly go back to him.

***

Auntie Rosalie called me several times. When I told her I had broken up with Claudio permanently, she was upset. She liked Claudio and didn't understand this at all. I guess she didn't want me passing up this opportunity to be happy.

I was so lost. But no matter what anyone said, I just couldn't take any more.

When I had left Nyx, I had told Claudio that my grandmother had hurt herself again and because my aunt couldn't get time off work a second time, I would go help out for a while. I didn't tell him what I had found out, because I knew he would somehow turn it all around and try to convince me to stay. I knew how easily he could make me feel sorry for him and how easily he could make me feel guilty about leaving him. And, in all honesty, at that point, I had not yet decided to break up with him. I couldn't make that decision then, because all my thoughts were so muddled up.

But in the letter I wrote him in Lausanne, I told him I did love him and always would, but explained that I needed to deal with this problem first. I still didn't want to hurt him. I told him that he could contact me if ever he needed me, even if it was ten or twenty years from now. I had told him that each time we had broken up. To me our relationship was still special, in the sense that I had wanted to sleep with only one man, and even now I had no intention of sleeping with many men in my life. Having sex with someone certainly did mean a lot to me, although with Claudio it hadn't been special at all. But I was still too weak to admit what had really happened between us physically. I couldn't face up to the fact that I had saved myself for a man like him, or, at least, bestowed what might have been left of my virginity on him.

I got an e–mail back from him, telling me that he would get back to me later, when he had the time. One of his friends from Switzerland was visiting him now. That hurt. And it had hurt, too, that he had been evasive and annoyed when I'd called him a few days before I wrote the letter. It sounded like he was involved with other matters and didn't want to spend much time with me on the phone. And this was the man who had claimed over and over again that he wanted to marry me!

Later, Carola and Elena told me the truth. I had been replaced. It shouldn't have surprised me, knowing how he felt about sex. He knew that I believed in being faithful to one man, but to him that meant nothing. "I like sex," I remembered him saying, making it sound as if it were just an activity like any other. But he knew what it meant to me.

I felt betrayed and was extremely upset by it. But even though his coolness hurt me, it never matched the pain of what he had done to me physically.

When I mentioned this in a phone call to Auntie Rosalie she didn't sympathize.

"What did you expect?" she asked. "You've obviously made up your mind. Do you expect him to beg? He gave you his heart and you just threw it away. You're the selfish, inconsiderate one here. I hope I can be that honest with you. Someone has to tell you the truth. You can't treat people this way. It isn't fair."

My guilt level kept going up, and I became increasingly frustrated and desperate. Was I really such an uncaring person? What had I done to deserve this? I couldn't make sense of anything anymore. I comforted myself with the thought that Auntie Rosalie didn't know the full story, the physical details and the lies, but I refused to change my mind about confiding in her. I was convinced that putting a permanent stop to the relationship I'd had with Claudio had been the right thing to do. That decision had been made, and I would not go back on it now, no matter what anyone said.

When I got back home from visiting my grandparents I went to see another psychiatrist, Irene. My experience with

Claudio had made me realize that I had to deal with this issue head on.

Chapter 5

This is when a very difficult period of my life began.

By the time I arrived home, Auntie Rosalie must have realized that I could no longer be strong enough to handle this alone. I had to get help, professional help. I believe my aunt tried to help me as best she could and had good intentions. After all, admitting that the niece she had raised needed to see a shrink couldn't have been easy.

A neighbor who was a psychiatrist had recommended I see Irene. She had written a letter, explaining what had happened to me. When I went to see Irene the first time, I gave her the letter and told her about my previous experience with a psychiatrist.

But Irene was so understanding, always supportive, never judging. Her deep, green eyes locked you in when she spoke, but fortunately she was also a good listener. Her long dark hair, which she mostly held out of her face with a hair band, and her slim figure made her pleasant to look at as well.

"The recovery will be difficult," she had said. "You will first get worse before you get better." She looked straight at me, keeping me in a grip with her eyes to make sure I understood very well that this was serious and that it would by no means be easy or over with quickly.

"I know," I said softly, looking down at my shoes, feeling terribly embarrassed about why I was there and about what I had done.

"Are you working right now?" she asked in a concerned, yet firm manner, picking up her notepad.

"I've just started a business degree course," I told her, not adding that I had enrolled purely out of survival instinct. A tiny part of me was not quite ready to throw in the towel, was still determined to get on with my life. But I had no idea where I was going or if I would actually make it there.

"I'm proud of you," she said with a smile, leaning back in her rattan armchair. "Many victims can't bring themselves to do anything constructive anymore, or they just go from one relationship to the next to find an answer, and always in vain."

"Nice lady," I thought, "but I suppose she has to say that to everyone to make them feel better."

But Irene didn't seem at all like the other psychiatrist I had seen before. She was open to my story. She listened. She cared about my recovery. It felt all right being there with her, dealing with this horrid secret. This deep lump that was sitting way down in my stomach needed to come out. I wanted that dreadful feeling inside of me to go away once and for all.

I admit that I was not completely convinced everything would work out after the first session, but the feeling I did have was far more positive than negative. And I had to face the fact that I wasn't dealing with this very well on my own, that I needed professional help.

At the time I wasn't taking any medication, and I told Irene I didn't want to.

"I want to do it without," I had said. "I want to be strong."

She agreed to that, saying that she thought I would most probably be all right without, for now, although it would have a calming effect on me, but if my condition worsened, she would insist that I take whatever she prescribed.

In our sessions, Irene often told me that I was too hard on myself. It actually felt good hearing that. I quite often would say things like, "I know I'm criticizing other people here, but I'm no saint either." That would get her going. She obviously felt that I needed a lot of reassuring. The fact that I had no faith in my own opinion would explain why I had been so easily influenced by my aunt's. This had to change.

Irene's office was a nice place to be: very homey and cozy, with a carpeted floor and some green leafy plants. And we sat in armchairs. I always felt warm and safe there.

I had started seeing Irene after my return from Switzerland. The first time I had called Irene for an appointment, I had to wait for three weeks since she had just returned from a holiday and had patients waiting. But when I had hung up the phone, I burst out into tears. I had waited so long already, and now I had to wait again. It took me some time to find the courage to call her again. I tried to convince myself it wouldn't be so bad to wait three more weeks. "It seems long now, but the three weeks will soon pass," is what I tried to get myself to believe. However, I was unable to convince myself of the latter, so I dried my tears and picked up the phone in the hallway.

She answered straight away. "Hi, this is Irene."

It was a relief not to hear the usual answering machine message and yet, when I heard her voice, I felt myself begin to falter. But I was determined. If I didn't speak now I would most certainly regret it later. Only when I heard my own voice did I realize that I had actually found the courage to speak.

"Hi, this is Elize again. I'm sorry to disturb you again, but there is no way I am going to make it through another three weeks on my own. I've already waited so long. I feel that I need help now." My voice was trembling, and I was trying very hard not to sob.

"I will need to go through my appointment book carefully to see when I can squeeze you in," she said in a soft but clear voice. "Give me some time to do that and I'll call you back."

I felt relieved and glad that I had called. I had been worried that by calling her again I might come across as a pushy person, someone who didn't show consideration for the patients who had been waiting to see her longer than I had. But the phone call had not appeared to concern her. She called me back a few hours later.

"Can you come see me next week?" she asked.

"Certainly," I said.

"Next week Friday at four?" she suggested.

"Terrific!" I sighed with relief. "Thank you so much," I said gratefully and hung up.

I felt much better. Finally there was a light at the end of the tunnel. It was still dim, but at least now I could see it.

During the following days, the anticipation of the appointment with Irene kept me going. Every time the situation was about to get the better of me, I focussed on the hand reaching out to me, Irene's hand, the hand that would help me with this ordeal.

Auntie Rosalie sympathized with me. She, too, was relieved that I could finally start my recovery.

She had called me at my grandparents' place two days before I was to return home and had just been to see the neighbor psychiatrist because, she told me, she had felt so helpless. For the first time since I'd arrived in Lausanne, I had the impression, from talking to her on the phone, that she just wanted to tell me that everything would be okay. But it wouldn't. Not just like that anyway. And she finally realized that. I think the neighbor psychiatrist had somehow been able to get her to grasp how serious the situation really was.

At first I saw Irene once a week. It was necessary to see her that often.

The first time I had gone, Auntie Rosalie had driven me there and waited in the waiting room. She had been worried I would be too upset to drive after my first session. But I was all right. So after that I always went by myself.

I never actually prepared myself for going to the appointments. Usually on the way over there, which took about forty–five minutes, I thought about what I would say to her. If there was something in particular that had come to me during the week I would write it down in order not to forget, but mostly that was not the case because my haunting thoughts and nightmares engraved themselves in my memory. The three–quarters of an hour's drive gave me enough time to figure out if there was anything else on my mind that needed to be dealt with then. Irene had given me her cell phone number so I could always call her if I needed to ask her anything in between the sessions. That was also comforting. She was only a phone call away.

The sessions lasted about an hour each time. We would start by going over my week. I would explain things that had happened, including bad dreams that I was having or everyday things that had triggered my memory of the rape. Sometimes it was something someone had said that had upset me. Other times, although there was nothing that caused me to remember the attack, I would suddenly feel very depressed.

I could feel so alone at times, so alone with my secret. Although others knew, it was and would always be my clandestine experience, my burden. After all, fundamentally I had to carry this alone. I suppose in a way you could compare it to dying. There may be someone holding your hand, but you're still taking the journey very much on your own.

During my first session with Irene, she had taken quite a few notes. By the next session she had listed several topics she wanted to discuss with me, although she made it clear that we didn't have to handle all those subjects during that second session. On the basis of my answers to her questions and other things that I had said during the first session, she had tried to establish which aspects of my life could have influenced how I was dealing with the trauma.

Irene told me that my personality had gone through a major change. I had shied away from myself, from the real me. I was denying myself the right to be true to myself. I was sacrificing myself, my talents, my ambitions. I had to get out of that vicious circle because it would only bring me down deeper and deeper.

And she was right. I felt as though I had fallen into a pit, one I couldn't get out of on my own. Furthermore, I was afraid of falling deeper. I did want to come out, but needed help and the right kind of help.

Irene took notes each time. She wasn't continually writing, so I did have eye contact with her practically throughout the entire session. It was all very personal.

I felt comfortable with her. You need to. Here is a stranger whom you are letting take charge of your mind and your life, giving her the power to play with your head. Come to think of it, it's pretty scary what kind of power you're handing over to this person. It's better not to dwell on it. But it is essential to be treated by someone you trust and someone who is capable of doing the job well.

At the beginning of the first few sessions I never really knew how to start or what to say. "You don't have to answer any questions or talk about anything you're not ready for," Irene told me reassuringly. "We will do this at your pace." Irene asked me questions about my family and about my childhood, questions that I suppose were mainly aimed at finding out who I was. Slowly but surely, we came to the conclusion that this traumatic experience had caused me to change my outlook on life completely.

"I think that the norms and standards you have always set for yourself have been lowered greatly," Irene commented during one of the sessions. "You don't respect yourself anymore, and therefore you don't command respect from others."

Usually after she had revealed a conclusion, she leaned back in her chair and crossed her legs. Often her stylish trousers or silk skirts would make me wonder where she shopped. But I knew I had to focus on what she had just said.

And she was right. I couldn't say I had ever been pretentious or arrogant, but I certainly had never been a pushover or indifferent to how other people treated me.

"Well, since the rape I always feel inferior and I easily feel guilty," I said hesitantly. "I feel as though I am always to blame."

"Yes," she said, nodding in agreement, turning over a page of her notepad. "And it's noticeable in several areas of your life, especially personal relationships. Are you experiencing any difficulties with the course you're taking? Are you able to handle it emotionally?"

"Well, the truth is, sometimes it does get rough," I admitted, feeling embarrassed about my weaknesses. "For no particular reason or because I suddenly think about the incident again without my mind being triggered by anything that I know of, I sometimes just can't hold back my tears."

I felt too guilty and ashamed to look at her. I swallowed loudly and continued.

"If it happens during class I try to cover my face by hiding behind my books or notepads, or I pretend to blow my nose and try to wipe away the tears with the tissue. Or if it becomes too much to handle, I go to the restroom."

Although it was difficult admitting to what I did, I knew that no matter what I told her she would never judge me, and that in itself brought me so much relief.

"I'm lucky that the lecturers often show slides so that the room is darker," I continued. "That way I feel a little more comfortable. I'm a little more invisible and my secret a little safer."

"Can you concentrate on the lessons?" she asked me.

"My mind wanders off at times," I admitted, now playing with my hair, twirling it around my fingers, feeling very self–conscious as I knew she was watching my each and every move. "I know I have to watch out for this so, when it happens, I try very hard to focus on something else, happy thoughts. But it doesn't always work."

It frightened me sometimes to think that I could no longer fool myself. I suppose that meant that therapy was working, and yet I felt insecure. And although I continued to try to fool others, I knew very well that I had to learn to live without believing in illusions.

"You know," I continued, blankly gazing in front of me, "even when I am able to hold everything inside during the class, it will all come pouring out afterward. At lunchtime I often walk over to a nearby park and sit behind a tree where no one can see me so I can cry. I cry so hard that my eyes are red and I wonder what people might be saying when I come back to class. But I try to cover up as much as I can."

I wanted her to tell me it would soon be over. But she had already warned me that it would be a long and difficult process. I could only hope that I had the courage to meet the challenge.

***

I had another concern that I kept quiet from everyone. The vaginal infection I had contracted in Greece didn't seem to want to go away, and I was worried. At the time, it hadn't been six months since I last slept with Claudio, and I knew that the HIV test could still turn out to be positive later on. So many things went through my head. Since he had slept with me without protection, perhaps he had done that with other girls as well, but I tried very hard to hang on to the hope that he hadn't, although hanging on to false hope was something that had become more and more difficult ever since I had started therapy. And, as a result, even though I had been to see Dr. Campbell when I got back from visiting my grandparents and he had given me an unguent and medication for the infection, I had begun to wonder if the reason why I wasn't getting better was because I had contracted HIV.

I kicked myself for being so careless. I had gone through this after having been raped in the Caribbean, but now I felt that it had been my own doing, even though I hadn't wanted to sleep with Claudio without protection. Perhaps the fact that I was now obsessing over the infection wasn't helping my recovery. I prayed time would pass quickly so that I would know for sure.

By the end of November I desperately needed a break. Auntie Rosalie agreed to let me go visit Nicholas, who was temporarily working in France on a project for the pharmaceutical company that had employed him, because she agreed with me that a change of scenery might do me good. She told Uncle Stephen that I had a week off from school to work on an assignment, and since I had always been a studious person in high school, he believed her when she said that I had finished the assignment ahead of time and, as a result, had a week of free time.

The stay with Nicholas did help although I had told him only briefly what had happened when I had returned home from Greece. Hearing that I had been raped, he took me in his arms and told me that he would always be there for me if I needed a listening ear. But we did not continue to talk about it, in part, because I felt so ashamed, but also, because, at the time, I hadn't known how to communicate to him how I was feeling.

Thinking back on that week at Nicholas', I realize that I must have driven him crazy. I even took up smoking because I needed something to calm me down. The entire week I felt as though I were going insane. I was exhausted and yet I couldn't sleep. I just broke down and cried a lot. I was shivering. I wasn't hungry. Images of the rape in the Caribbean and of those nights with Claudio kept appearing before me like a movie trailer. They never stopped, and I was afraid to close my eyes to sleep.

I also started drinking gin to calm myself down a little, although it didn't help. And I was careful. I tried to be responsible even in the midst of this madness.

I asked Nicholas if he would let me try cannabis. So one evening we went to the park where there were dealers, but they didn't have any cannabis that night. I didn't feel comfortable trying anything else — I wasn't even too sure about cannabis at the time.

I went to bed that night, leaving the lights on, hoping the drowsiness I now experienced from the alcohol was a sign that I would be able to get some sleep.

That night I dreamed that Claudio was on top me, his sweat dripping on me. We had just had sex, but he had wanted to do it a second time. During the second time he humped me like his life depended on it. He was this hideous creature on top of me, pleasing himself to get an orgasm. His back, neck and hair were wet. I was disgusted. I lay there beneath him, wishing he'd come soon so that it would be over. I felt so filthy. I hated it so much. Finally he came. I pushed him away from me. He had what he wanted. I didn't want his sweaty body touching me anymore. He didn't understand that. He just lay there so contented. He made me so sick. I truly felt nauseated. The mere sight of him was repulsive. I had no idea I was capable of loathing someone as much as I loathed him.

I woke up sweating and began to cry. I looked at the alarm clock. It was only three o'clock, but I didn't want to go back to sleep. Although, even awake, I could see their faces, Claudio's and that of the Caribbean rapist, who had now detached himself from my former fiancé, and whom I, in an attempt to get rid of, seemed to have cloned. Because, instead of one unwanted companion, I now had two.

As strange as it may sound, before the incident I would tell boys if I didn't particularly like the way they kissed me: if their tongue twirling annoyed me, or if they were just too slobbery. I was fearless. I just said what I had to say. The guy had to get it right if he wanted to kiss me. I'd leave a date early if I got bored. But now I just put up with anything and everything, no matter how repugnant it was to me.

After the attack in the Caribbean and before I met Claudio I had regularly thought of having a one–night stand. I wasn't a virgin anymore anyway, and I had come to believe that, by having sex, I could undo the rape. But after the episode with Claudio, I couldn't even watch sex scenes on TV anymore. Sex had become anything but beautiful and special. When Claudio had raved about having such great orgasms, I had often literally felt sick.

I remembered the evening before I left for Switzerland. Claudio had said to me, "I guess Pam and her five friends are going to have to do it for me now." Obviously he meant masturbating. I felt that that was all he had ever needed me for, which would explain why I had been so quickly replaced, although by someone who, according to Carola's letter, was very much her own woman and who often stood him up. But, at that moment, even though I found that the thought of it disgusted me, I was too relieved that I was leaving to make a big deal out of it.

***

On the third day of my stay with Nicholas we had gone to get groceries and were driving back home when, suddenly, he asked me if Claudio and I had used condoms.

That caught me by surprise. "Where did that come from?" I asked indignantly.

I think I was so offended because he was implying that I was either a stupid or a careless person, and I expect he must have seen my reaction reflected in my expression when he glanced at me.

"Well, you said you had an infection," he replied, checking his rearview mirror. "So, did you use a condom?"

I had told him about the infection that morning after he had seen me taking an unguent into the bathroom. Nicholas had a science degree and was working for a pharmaceutical company, so I didn't think fooling him would work long.

"What does that have to do with anything?" I demanded angrily, suddenly near tears. Because I knew that it had everything to do with everything. I had put myself in danger.

Not intentionally. But I had placed my trust in Claudio, and now I knew what a fool I had been.

"Well, if you don't use one, you can catch diseases," Nicholas answered me, changing gears. "Including AIDS. You must know that."

"Even if you use a condom you can still catch diseases," I snapped back, defending myself. I was upset and hurt, and now crying bitterly.

"Yes, I suppose so," he said, "but it's highly unlikely. Anyway, you knew this guy, right?"

"It is still possible, even with a condom," I repeated, searching for a tissue in my pocket, not knowing what else to say. I couldn't tell him how terrified I was that I had contracted an incurable disease from Claudio, even though I had never given him my consent to have sex without protection.

The truth was, I felt that I didn't know Claudio at all. I could never be sure if he had used condoms with the other girls he had been with. I sincerely doubted it. Because if during the times with the other girls, he hadn't felt any sensation, he probably would have removed the condom when he was with them, too. For all I knew he had always lied and never used one at all.

I felt that in Nicholas' and Auntie Rosalie's opinion I had now been reduced to the problem child who had clearly made a mess of things.

But I decided to confide in Nicholas all the same. So later that day I attempted to tell him what it had really been like with Claudio, concluding with the nightmare I'd had.

We were sitting next to one another on wobbly wooden stools at the kitchen table in Nicholas' one-bedroom apartment.

"I know that even for a boyfriend it is difficult to keep on being supportive," he said, stroking me over my hair, "but from what you're telling me it sounds like Claudio used your body to jerk himself off."

Hearing that made me cry. The truth hurt badly. Until then I had allowed myself to believe it hadn't been that bad. I always blamed myself for not enjoying sex. But the full realization that Claudio had simply used me as a sexual object was a hard blow to take.

"Unfortunately, it seems that few men care enough and are selfless enough to be understanding and supportive of women," Nicholas continued. "I met Claudio. He had us all fooled. That's the sad truth."

"He put on this façade to the outside world which made it so much more difficult for me to face what he was really like," I sobbed, brushing away my tears. "We did have communication problems. That is, he never took notice of anything I said. But with everyone telling me how sweet and caring he was, what could I think?"

"I know. It's not your fault," Nicholas said soothingly, pinching my chin gently. "He fooled us all."

I continued to cry and Nicholas held me, telling me over and over again that it would be okay.

Finally, for the first time, someone was telling me that everything would be all right. I had been craving to hear those words for such a long time, but, now that I heard them at last, I had reached the stage where I could no longer fool myself into believing them.

At the back of my mind, I had always worried about the fact that I couldn't be certain that Claudio was free of disease. He had taken me as though it were his right, holding my arms when I tried to push him away, opening my legs with his knee when I struggled to get away from him, even when I told him, over and over again, that he was hurting me. But I couldn't tell Nicholas that.

But I wondered now, not for the first time, how I could have been such a fool as to let Claudio use me that way. He had made me feel like a waste disposal, so incredibly filthy and low that now I did not even want to look at my own body. I couldn't love it anymore after what had happened to it.

Nicholas advised me not to try to shut the experiences out of my mind. Whenever he sensed that I couldn't take any more, he would say, "I can tell you're going crazy, but you have to face what you experienced once and for all, no matter how painful it is. You tell me you keep seeing fragments of what you endured in St. Catherine's and in Nyx. Well, you should look at those images, instead of pushing them away, because only if you truly know what happened to you, can you start dealing with it all."

Although, during my stay with Nicolas, the first specter had reappeared, and from then on I had two specters who accompanied me, I knew that now that the Caribbean monster was out of his hiding spot, I could finally start dealing with what he had done to me, and only then could I try to comprehend what had happened in Nyx. Being with my cousin had certainly helped me, if for no other reason than my realizing that Irene was right. It had to get worse, much worse, before it got better.

**

When I was back from visiting Nicholas, Irene insisted I take something, even if it was only herbal medicine to enable me to get some sleep, because I was exhausted. And so I started taking pills containing extracts of valerian, hops and passionflower.

I also started reading books about relationships and about sex. Some parts were quite confrontational. The articles about why men rape were especially difficult to read. But I was determined to do something to overcome my fear.

Whenever I went for my appointment, Irene asked me what I had been up to, and I had been quite proud of having made myself read that material. I suppose I believed I had to suffer first and face my fears, on any level really, before I could heal, sort of like forcing myself to be with Claudio, seeing that as an unfortunate necessity I had to go through before I could be cured.

"Why are you so often forcing yourself to be so confrontational?" Irene asked me in a rather concerned tone in our next session.

"I guess that's just me," I said, shrugging my shoulders. "I thought that reading about these things might help me."

But I had finally begun to face reality. And it was painful. All these memories were coming to me in no particular order. And I had to put all the bits and pieces together, examining each one as an individual part of the puzzle. The Caribbean rapist. Claudio. Everything was muddled up. How was I to come to any peace of mind with a head like mine? Thinking gave me a headache. But I was determined to see it through.

As the assault in the Caribbean had been blocked out for a long time there were parts I couldn't remember. They may have been lost forever. But those lost memories were not what was most important.

After I had managed to put the pieces in place and play the scenario of the rape, to let myself see it and experience it again, I found some inner rest. I knew that what had happened to me in St. Catherine's had not been my fault, because I had told him to stop over and over again. Discovering that came as a great relief to me. Unfortunately, this did not mean that I didn't feel guilty anymore.

Nina Holden

I suppose that the fact that I had blocked out the rape for so long made dealing with it now so much more difficult. And I now also had to account for my behavior after the attack: the secrecy, the lies, and, more importantly, everything that had happened with Claudio.

I often felt that I didn't want to live anymore. I could cry for hours, and I always cried myself to sleep. I would put on music to fall asleep with. The music had to be chosen carefully as certain phrases could trigger a memory or feeling.

One evening, feeling particularly depressed, I went for a walk outside, crying. I felt like a tap no one could close. The stores in the village were closed, and there were only a few people about. Suddenly, I knew I couldn't walk straight anymore. I lay down on the sidewalk. People walking by stared but didn't speak to me. They must have thought that I was someone who had lost her mind completely.

I felt a sense of complete despair. I had never sunk this deep. I wanted to go lie down in the middle of the street so that someone would drive over me and it would finally all be over.

After I had made it back home, I had two strong drinks. Since I didn't drink that much alcohol this was enough to make me fall asleep. I stumbled up the stairs and went to bed.

But the next morning I realized what I had done and was frightened by it. What I remembered of the previous evening didn't sound at all like me. So, then and there, I made a pact with myself that I would always stay in control of my own actions from then on. Because I couldn't permit myself to get out of hand like that ever again. But, considering the unstable state I was in, I knew that the challenge I was facing was not one that I could afford to underestimate.

142

***

After having gone through hell and back trying to remember as much as I could from everything I had been through, I was now in a better position to talk to Irene about how my personality had been affected.

I told her that I had become someone I did not want to be. I had once thought that being afraid was an exercise of futility and that I should never look back on a decision and say, "If only…" Now I had regrets. I questioned everything I had ever done. I even found myself wishing sometimes that I'd had sex when I'd been much younger so that the rape would not have been my first experience with it.

Irene often gave me advice about how to live day by day.

"You need to stand up for yourself," Irene said repeatedly, trying to get the message into my head.

As I usually did when she gave me advice, I nodded and said, "I know. But I feel so worthless, and I have felt this way ever since the attack in St. Catherine's. I feel as though I don't matter anymore. And even when I try to convince myself that I do, someone like Claudio comes along and makes it all so much worse."

"After a traumatic experience it's much harder to set your personal boundaries and stick to them," Irene said, giving me that strong hard look which meant: *believe me, I know what I'm talking about.* "It's a common phenomenon among rape victims to let other people cross them much more easily. And concerning what happened with Claudio, you are certainly not an isolated case."

Hearing that came as a relief. "I know that doesn't excuse his behavior, but it makes me feel less guilty about being so weak," I replied, dropping back in the armchair, looking down to avoid her glance as I knew what was coming next.

"You're being too hard on yourself again," she said, leaning forward to emphasize the importance of what she was saying. And it was something she had said to me several times before.

"Knowing that other people who have had similar experiences make the same mistakes afterward helps. It makes me feel less of a fool," I said in my own defense.

"Surely there were happy times too in that relationship," Irene said, still leaning forward. "After all, you did agree to sleep with him."

"He wanted to marry me," I said, "and he was willing to put up with me, with the fact that I had no experience, with the fact that I had been raped. I thought I should be grateful that he put up with me," I said to her.

"But you said he enjoyed the sex," she said. "It doesn't sound like he was putting up with you."

And it was true. He had never complained about the sex. While I saw it as a necessary burden, one that I should carry until my dues had been paid and I could finally be free, he always thought that it was great and was only annoyed when I brought up my problems with it. And since Auntie Rosalie had told me I would never find a guy who loved me as much as Claudio and that no man could ever understand anything like rape, I was even more inclined to be thankful to Claudio for putting up with me and my situation.

"Isn't that what you said then?" Irene asked.

There was, as always, empathy in her eyes. I had the feeling that she understood me better than I did myself.

Later, walking down the street to the car, I was struck by the realization that, for some reason, I had eventually been strong enough to get out of my relationship with a man who did not respect me and that I should be proud of that.

And, for the first time in more that two years, I was. When I had truly been worn out, somehow I had found the courage that I had lacked before and had been able to save myself from the awful fate I was heading toward, a fate so dreadful, that even now, I didn't dare to imagine it. Similar to a person dying, at the very last moment, I'd had a brief revival. Yet my revival didn't lead to death, but to the road of resurrection.

***

Irene certainly did help me see things from a different perspective. She helped me boost my self–confidence, my self–esteem and dignity, convincing me that I needed to learn to like myself again. And I needed to forgive. Auntie Rosalie had said that the neighbor psychiatrist had told her I first had to forgive the rapist before I could carry on. Irene disagreed. She said it was okay to hate him for what he did to me. But I had to forgive myself, to tell myself that it was okay. I could accept that a lot better. I had to forgive myself to get rid of all that guilt. Without forgiving myself I could never carry on. Not all the guilt is gone, but that very hard but first step of forgiveness was essential.

Irene was always patient with me. I did ask her questions she couldn't answer since, unfortunately, psychiatrists do not have crystal balls they can consult to give you advice on how to lead a life that is free from all harm. During some sessions I just wanted to keep asking, just drain her for information. That was also due to my lack of self–confidence. I trusted her opinion a lot more than mine.

Irene had firmly stated that I should not dismiss the fact that Claudio and I had serious communication problems and that I let him use me and make me do things I was very

Nina Holden

unhappy with, and that was indeed a result of my traumatic experience. Ignoring my wishes not to offer Matt alcohol and expecting me to pay for practically everything while his money went to his ex–wife were two ways in which I had let him cross my boundaries.

Irene said it was very important that the next time I established a relationship, it should be based on trust and mutual respect. Only then should I take the step to have a physical romance. Snuggling up close together should feel comfortable and pleasant. I would have to be completely convinced that if at any moment I wanted to stop, while having sex, this should be possible and exactly what should happen. And I made up my mind that, no matter what, the next time I would stick to what I had asked Claudio to do in Nyx: I would take things one step at a time. And this time, *I* would not take no for an answer.

Chapter 6

Charlene called me the Saturday afternoon right after the last day of my first year in college. She had just started working for an export company, her first job after her very recent graduation from the University of Pennsylvania. As I was home and didn't have anything planned for the evening yet, we agreed to go see a movie.

Since Charlene was late, I bought the tickets and was waiting for her when she arrived, apologizing for her tardiness. We rushed to the theater where we found two seats near the back, and after a few commercials the film began.

After about half an hour, a teenage girl in the movie asked her mother if she had washed her black dress. The mother replied that she hadn't been able to because the machine was broken and that she had called a repairman to come over to fix it. That was all but it was enough. I couldn't breathe.

Whispering to Charlene that I really had to go, I rushed to the restroom, which, fortunately, was empty. Going into a stall, I locked the red door behind me. Standing with my back against it, I tried to catch my breath. Tears of anguish were running down my cheeks. Why could I still not handle this?

Finally, I left the stall, hoping that I could control myself enough to keep from breaking into sobs again. Although Charlene knew what had happened to me in the Caribbean, I still preferred to make up lies again, about not feeling well, so awful in fact that I would cry because of it, because being considered pathetic and childish was always better than admitting to the awful truth that the memory of the rape could still put me in the state I was in now. When would I get my life back? I knew, of course, that I would never get it back. I would have to take it back. "Okay, take a deep breath," I told myself, "and you'll be all right! Believe it, at least until you're in bed tonight and you're alone. Alone with your burden."

I managed to clean up my face a bit. I dreaded going back to the theater, and for the remainder of the film I felt uneasy to say the least. But I got through it.

At times like those, I blamed myself for letting the incident continue to play such a big part in my life. On the one hand, I realized I should cut myself some slack. It would always be a sensitive subject. I was stuck with that. On the other hand, I just wished I wasn't.

After the movie had finished, we left the theater and strolled over to Martin's Coffee House across the road. The film had started at five–thirty, and we hadn't had a chance to talk since Charlene had been running late.

"So, how have you been?" she asked me with an enormous smile, obviously trying to perk me up.

Charlene looked very attractive in tight blue jeans and a short, brown, V–neck sweater, with her soft pink lips and eyes skillfully outlined in black. Clearly she took pride in her appearance. As for me, I was wearing brown drawstring trousers and a baggy black shirt. I didn't bother with make–up anymore. Because my body had been sexually abused, I thought of it as being blemished. It was as though there were deep stains on it that would never come out. I didn't even want to live in my body anymore, let alone take care of it. What was the point of being beautiful now? I wasn't anymore and never would be again.

"I'm all right," I said faintly.

Actually I was depressed. After the rape I had started eating more. Trying to eat the pain and distress away, I had put on about thirty pounds. Although I now felt fat and ugly, in a strange way, I felt safer. Perhaps it was because I knew that I was no longer as attractive to men. But looking at Charlene, I was aware of the fact that I actually wanted to make a new start, to have a new body, a new chance, a new life. I didn't want what I had made of my life since the rape.

"I wanted to talk to you," Charlene continued, putting down her coffee.

"What about?" I asked her, instantly alert. Charlene never spoke this way unless she had something serious on her mind. But I was in no mood for anything that required much thought. In fact, all I truly wanted to do was to have a coffee and to try to relax a bit after that awful episode in the theater.

"Well, you know," she whispered, "your situation. The R thing."

She must have seen the puzzled look on my face. We usually talked about how I was feeling and what I had done, but apart from the time that I had told her I'd been attacked, we hadn't spoken about it in any more depth.

"What about it?" I asked, hoping that Charlene wouldn't stay on the subject for long. Although I realized that we had never discussed the rape much, she had picked a lousy time to bring it up. I had been able to keep it together for the remainder of the movie, but I knew that because the memory of the rape had been triggered while watching the film, not much would be needed for me to break down and begin to cry again.

"I think you should talk to Holly," she said.

"Is she a shrink?" I inquired in a rather sharp tone. Didn't Charlene know that I was already seeing one?

"No," Charlene said. "Holly is also a victim. I think you two should talk. I'm sure it would help."

"How do you know?" I asked her. Since I was deeply ashamed of what had happened to me and, as a result, had confided in very few people, I wondered how Charlene had found out that this girl had been raped, too.

"Well," she began, "I know you don't want to go to a self–help group, so maybe talking to her, sharing experiences and all —"

"No, that's not what I meant," I interrupted. I looked around and then added in a lower voice, "How do you know she's a victim?"

"She's my brother's girlfriend," Charlene said. "He told me."

"Does Holly want to talk to me?" I asked.

"Yes, Dave says she does," Charlene replied.

"Dave knows?" I asked anxiously.

"Don't worry," she said reassuringly. "I only told Dave after he told me about Holly. I only told him because I thought I could help. Please don't be mad. I swore him to secrecy."

I smiled at her. Of course I couldn't be mad. How could I ever be angry with someone who wanted to help me so badly?

"I'm not mad," I said. "Thanks for caring."

"Of course I care," she replied.

I knew I could never face Dave again, but we'd never been close anyway. But wow, another victim wanted to talk to me!

"I think it would help," Charlene continued, putting her hand over mine.

"Okay," I said. "But I don't want too many people knowing about this."

"I promise I won't tell another soul," Charlene reassured me, crossing her heart, the way we had made promises as children.

We hugged right there across the table. The world around us no longer existed. At least not for me. Charlene was my guardian angel. I could now talk to another victim without having to tell my story to a room full of strangers. Now I could talk to a girl named Holly, someone who could really understand me.

We changed the subject at my request, and Charlene began to tell me all about her new job. But I couldn't pay as much attention to her story as I should have. The encounter with Holly was what occupied my mind.

Charlene had to leave around ten.

"Listen, I'll give Holly your number so she can give you a call," she said as we crossed the street back to our cars.

I was surprised at how excited I was. Although I knew there were groups in which people who had been assaulted discussed their problems, even now, that still seemed like too public a forum for me. But perhaps talking to a woman on a one to one basis was something I could handle, something that might offer relief, the kind of relief that even Irene had not been able to give me.

***

The very next morning, around eleven, Holly gave me a call. Auntie Rosalie picked up the phone in the hallway.

"It's for you," she called loudly into the living room. "It's a girl named Holly."

I got up from the brown leather sofa, put down the magazine I was reading, stubbing my toe against the coffee table as I rushed out to the hallway.

"Hello Holly," I said, trying to sound as matter of fact as possible.

"Hello," she said. "I got your number from Charlene."

Holly spoke slowly and clearly, articulating every word. Although I knew practically nothing about her, I immediately felt encouraged. She did not sound like a victim at all. She sounded kind, but strong.

"Most of next week will be difficult for me to meet with you," she said, "but you could come over this evening around six, if you're not doing anything."

I realized that Charlene must have told her I wasn't doing much of anything these days. But that was all right. It would only be several more hours now until I could talk to someone who had endured my pain, too.

That evening, I left early, not wanting to be late. Holly and Dave lived in a freshly renovated one–bedroom apartment, about a twenty–minute drive from our house. He worked in advertising, and she was employed as a business consultant.

Because of Charlene, I had met Dave a few times, but I barely knew him. He was a tall, handsome, dark–haired, muscular fellow who played basketball, the kind of man any woman would haven been proud of. I wondered how Holly had met him. Certainly he was no Claudio, at least from what I had seen, although I should have known then that what people seemed to be was often something quite different from what they really were, and I only hoped that Holly had chosen more wisely than I had and that she was happy.

I pressed on the buzzer, and Holly answered. The heavy black doors of the apartment building unlocked, and I pushed them open using the full weight of my body. It was clearly fat that made me heavier, not muscle.

"Come on in," she said, opening the door to her apartment. Holly looked about my age in her blue jeans and red cotton top, but since Dave was twenty–eight, I thought that she would be more his age. "Dave's not here," she added. "He's coaching basketball."

Relieved, I smiled and handed her my coat, which she hung up in a built–in wardrobe by the door. Walking over to the beige sofa in the living room, we passed the dining room and I noticed a vase with about a dozen white roses on the table. Dave must have given them to her. What a sweetheart! But then again, perhaps Holly didn't even like white roses. Perhaps Dave *was* like Claudio, and as he had always given me the kind of chocolate I didn't like, perhaps Dave had given Holly the kind of flowers she didn't like, and like me, she just put up with it, kidding herself that he was thoughtful.

"Would you like a drink, or some cookies? There's plenty left over. Dave bought them for my birthday last week, but we never ate many. I hate birthdays. Twenty–seven. I wonder what I've been doing all those years."

Maybe the flowers had been for her birthday, too.

"I'd like some water," I replied in a shy soft–spoken voice, "but no cookies." She had such a slim figure, and I felt fat. She walked gracefully. Her sleek brown shoulder–length hair swayed as she moved. Holly appeared to have overcome this trauma. I had to at least make it look like I was making an effort.

But now I knew how old she was. And we were very similar. That is, I hated birthdays for the precise reason she had just mentioned.

During one of my sessions, I had told Irene that I felt that I very clearly lacked ambitions now.

"I wouldn't say you lack them completely," she had replied. "You may not have them as much as before, but the fact that you're doing a degree course clearly means that you're determined to get on with your life. You may not realize it, but considering what you've been through, that is something to be proud of. Sometimes victims can't bring themselves to do anything. You should feel good about yourself for that. Well done!" Leaning back in her rattan armchair she added, "Why *aren't* you proud of yourself then?"

Her questions were always penetrating. She made me think, often when I didn't want to because the answers were so painful.

I knew very well that the course did not represent a new start for me. I had no aspirations whatsoever. I did not want to go further in that field. It seemed that I had to fill my time with something, anything. Even though I had no dreams, no ambitions, I felt that I was only making things worse by wasting time. No matter what had happened to me, no matter how meaningless life seemed now, I had to be useful. The thought of life just going on without me actually doing something in it was too awful to accept. It was almost as if my personal resume had to be filled up. There could be no blanks. Everything had to be justified.

And, like Holly, I was reminded of that every birthday. I'd become a year older, but I never seemed to have accomplished anything. Even when I was little, there were so many things I wanted to have done before a certain age.

Holly returned with the water and sat down beside me. But then she let herself sink into the sofa and her arms were left dangling. She had made a very different impression when I'd entered the apartment. Now that I looked more closely, I could see that she was not as self–assured as I had thought. Obviously, she, too, still suffered. I could see it in her eyes.

"It's hard, isn't it?" I began. I hoped she wouldn't take this to mean that I thought she hadn't coped. But I saw at once that I hadn't upset her.

"It will always be hard," she replied, laying her head back on the sofa. "Dealing with it together with another person, someone special, makes it easier, but you can do it on your own. Ultimately you have to heal yourself. No one can do that for you."

Her look told me: *that's how it is, kid.*

And then she began to tell me about her own rape. It had happened on a short trip to France, a prize that she had been awarded at high school graduation as best student in her French class. She'd been eighteen at the time and had traveled alone. One of the hotel staff had come into her room in the middle of the night when she was in bed.

Holly didn't want to disclose the details, and I respected that.

I told her my story. She listened carefully. Likewise, I did not reveal all the details.

"Do you have a boyfriend now?" she asked after a brief moment of respectful silence, although she must have known from Charlene that I didn't.

I shook my head. "I did have one afterward though," I told her, "but it was horrible. I hated it."

"What happened?" she asked in a rather curious tone, biting her bottom lip in an uneasy manner.

I realized that there was a mutual unspoken understanding that we would only disclose what we felt comfortable with. But I still felt so ashamed, even with her. After all, we didn't even know one another. And perhaps that was for the best, because it had been less embarrassing to talk to Irene about everything that had happened to me than to people to whom I was close, and she had been a stranger, too. I did realize that Irene was a therapist, but, then again, Holly and I had experienced the same horrible intrusion.

"One of the problems in the relationship was that I hated Claudio touching me in public," I began my story, becoming aware of the pain these memories always brought with them. "We had broken up for that very reason for a while. He just kept at it and when I said that our relationship was over he said I hadn't even given it a decent try. Other couples were all over each other, so we should be, too."

"You know," Holly said, "your not wanting him to touch you all the time turns out to be a normal reaction. Other girls I have spoken to who were raped couldn't stand it either. They also didn't want to sleep with their boyfriends much. When they did they didn't enjoy it, but at the time they didn't know any better and didn't give much attention to the fact that they didn't enjoy it. Quite often they had to stop during sex because something triggered their memory. And when they didn't want to make love, their boyfriends would accuse them of using the rape as an excuse. Unfortunately you don't always have those people around you when you need them. Talking to other victims taught me that it is possible to be happy again, but it takes time and you have to work through it."

But, wait a minute. Had I heard this right? Was there hope after all? I didn't know if Holly was really talking about other people or indirectly about herself. But that didn't matter. She had given me hope. Finally, for the first time since the attack, someone had actually been able to give me hope.

"Are you all right now, with Dave?" I asked her, hoping she would know that I hadn't asked out of curiosity, but rather because of genuine concern.

When she assured me that she was, I was so happy for her and it made me hopeful for my future. Perhaps it would be all right to believe that I could still have a wonderful relationship with a man. Surely, this was not yet another illusion I would try to hold on to, in vain.

The fact that she had been so frank with me made it easier for me to tell her about Claudio.

"He wanted to get married soon and have children," I began. "That was probably what made me trust him. But he didn't meet any of the standards I had set for a husband. And he was not a child: he was thirty. I actually thought I had made a good choice going out with an older man because he should be more experienced and more understanding. I believed an older man would show more respect for my situation. But once we were in a serious relationship, I didn't want to be with him. I just wanted to run away, to get as far away from him as possible. I don't know how I could have stayed with him that long. Actually we broke up a few times, so I suppose we weren't together as long as that. I kept trying to run away, you see."

"You're not the only one who has done that," Holly reassured me. "There have been a lot of us. Believe me."

I wondered how Holly could know that unless she really had spoken with other victims. Perhaps she had been strong enough to go to a self–help group. But I could see that my story struck a chord with her. Suddenly she looked self–conscious. She cleared her throat.

"I wanted to get away from my boyfriend as well," Holly admitted, "the one prior to Dave, but for some reason I just kept going back to him."

She now looked at me with the exact same expression I knew I had often worn when I talked with Irene. Now, seeing it on someone else's face, I immediately recognized it for what it was. Holly was confessing, just as I had been when I had admitted my guilt and shame to Irene.

"I didn't love him at all," Holly continued bravely, her brown eyes wet with unshed tears. "I did it because I thought that being alone was worse than being with him."

She looked at me, clearly asking for reassurance. "I know," I said in a soft voice. It was important to tell her that she wasn't alone either.

"When I was by myself," she said, "I had to deal with everything on my own. He provided distraction."

It was obvious that it hadn't been easy for her to get to the stage in her life where she was now. And that she, too, had made mistakes.

"We'd separate," she sobbed, "but I kept going back to him."

My eyes were wet, too, now. But I wanted to comfort her in some way. I was extremely grateful to her for revealing to me that even after having been raped, there was still a chance that all would be well again at some point in my life. She had given me something to look forward to again, and I wanted so much to show her how much I appreciated what she had done for me.

I put my hand on Holly's shoulder as she took a tissue from her pocket and dried her eyes.

"I'm all right," she assured me.

But it was clear that she still felt a lot of pain. I realized that, even though Holly seemed so self–possessed, it would take both of us a long time to recover from what neither of us could ever deny. We had been violated. And something inside us would never be the same.

Chapter 7

I had fewer nightmares now, and the haunting images of what I had endured, that I still saw quite frequently, would begin to fade into the distance faster. I had stopped seeing Irene two months earlier, after having been in therapy with her for about nine months, and was no longer taking herbal medicine. But who was I kidding? I was much better, but I couldn't diagnose myself as fully cured. I was not always in control of my emotions. A particular incident or phrase in a song could cause me to break down and cry at any given moment. And I still couldn't watch certain films or read particular books.

How much longer would this last? Would the time ever come when, around any corner, nothing would be waiting to trigger those terrible memories? When would I be able to get on with my life? The mere thought of the rape still cut like a knife, and I still looked for ways to compensate for it. But, of course, I couldn't. I guess the fact that I was still trying to erase the rape from my existence showed that I hadn't accepted it.

In a way, I hoped that my next sexual encounter would be my true first time. Irene had told me that I still hadn't had real sex and that my first actual experience with it would be when I'd sleep with a man and discover the beauty of making love and enjoy it, as opposed to being used and abused. Maybe I was kidding myself, but it was the only way I could think of to start afresh.

I tried to hold on to the hope that Holly had given me, that it was still possible to be happy, even after having been through an ordeal like mine. But I did worry that if I didn't enjoy my next experience with sex, I would go off it for life.

In fact, I was still so tormented by what I had endured that I tried to be open to practically anything that might help. I assume it was mainly out of this fear of being hurt by men that I tried to convince myself to try homosexuality, thinking that if I were a lesbian I would not have to go through penetration while having sex. I could just be touched, caressed and loved without there ever having to be a penis present. I tried to fantasize about it, and I paid extra attention to good–looking women whom I might find attractive. But the sexual attraction simply wasn't there and, finally, I was forced to come to the sad conclusion that if I were to have sex at all, it would have to be with a man.

I suppose that it was only natural that I would try to find an instant solution, even if it involved making me into someone I was not. And I secretly still hoped that maybe if I just enjoyed sex once I would be cured, although I knew very well that I had to heal myself. No one could do it for me. I was just so desperate. I suppose I didn't know what I was thinking anymore.

So although I had stopped seeing Irene, I decided to make a new appointment to discuss my concerns. I wanted to ask her more practical questions about how other people deal with sex after a rape experience. I was convinced there was a clear difference if the rape was your first sexual experience, and I needed advice that would put my mind at rest.

I was happy I could still see her before my summer holidays ended and it was time to go back to school. I had done some temporary work as a receptionist at a learning center for ten days to earn some extra money. But other than that I had spent most of my time just relaxing, hanging out with friends, and reading.

Two weeks later, I drove to my appointment, feeling embarrassed about what I wanted to ask Irene. But once I was there, I told her that I was still so afraid of making the same mistake as I had with Claudio and needed more advice on how to deal with a future sexual relationship.

"My advice is to just take it one step at a time," she told me. "Don't do anything you're not comfortable with. But it's difficult to give you exact advice because every individual is different and has different needs. I wish I could give you a set of rules to follow, but life doesn't work that way. You're going to have to decide what's right for you and what isn't."

Although I knew very well that what she had just said made sense, it wasn't enough to stop me from worrying.

"So, it will always be a risk," I said. "I don't think I'll survive if I ever have to go through what I've been through, again."

"Trust your own instincts, and don't rush into anything," Irene said. "Try to feel comfortable with someone first, and make sure you can communicate well and that the man respects you. You're much stronger now than you were when you met Claudio, don't forget that."

Perhaps I was much stronger, but I realized very well that I could still easily be brought to tears or made to feel despair. But I also knew that Irene had answered my question as best she could.

"Does being raped without prior sexual experience make a difference?" I asked her, wondering if she would confirm what I had assumed.

161

"Well," Irene began, "a negative first experience makes it much more difficult to feel comfortable with sex and overcome the first experience. A previous positive experience makes it easier. Then you are comforted by the knowledge that something else, something much better, is possible. Without this positive experience there is only hope, no knowledge of anything better. Quite often one first negative experience is followed by so many negative others that you become caught in a vicious circle. But you've had therapy, Elize, and I think you're strong enough to make rational decisions now. And remember, you can always come to see me or call me if you need more help."

"Thank you," I said, comforted by the thought that Irene was a kind of safety net I could always fall back on.

Although this appointment had not given me the solace I was looking for, it did make me realize how blessed I was, having someone like her who I could always turn to for encouragement. I will always be grateful to her and think myself lucky, lucky that my insecurities and endless questions had not driven her mad.

Irene had only been able to reassure me a bit, but little did I know that my salvation lay just several hours away.

I left Irene's office around four and headed for the library where I had signed up earlier that day to use the Internet at five, since the computer at home had crashed the night before. While I was there, I would pick up a video for Nicholas.

The library was a newly renovated building with wide stairs that led up to an area where five computers were available for public use. I walked over to the computer I had reserved, sat down and logged in.

I had received a short e–mail from Charlene, sent that morning, asking me if I was interested in going to a party that weekend and saying that she would call me later. I replied that I would not be checking my e–mail regularly since our computer had crashed and that it was, indeed, better to call.

Then I checked my junk mail, because sometimes certain e–mails that I did want to receive had ended up there. Not for the first time, I came across e–mails entitled "rape sex." I never opened them, of course, but the mere word "rape" was enough to upset me, especially when it was associated with sex. I was still trying very hard to convince myself that the two had nothing to do with each other. How people could associate rape with sex, a word that should imply nothing but pleasure, was beyond me. I didn't even want to hear the explanation. Just knowing that there were people out there with no real understanding of what was, after all, a crime distressed me.

Having checked my e–mail, I headed for the video section to get Nicholas' thriller. On the way to the checkout counter, I looked through the library's collection, skimming the titles. And then, before realizing that I was walking past the travel videos, I suddenly stood face to face with the Caribbean island where my life had changed forever.

I don't know how long I stood there staring at the picture of the island on the box of that video, but I only became aware of what I was doing when an elderly man asked to get through.

"Sure," I said disconcerted, moving out of his way and proceeding to check out the thriller.

Once I was home, I ran up to my room and threw myself on my bed. I had managed to keep it together for the drive home, but now everything just came pouring out.

Although my condition and state of mind had improved, I clearly had to face facts. I had not recovered completely. I was constantly reminded of that. Even now, every time the memory of the rape was triggered, I became greatly distressed. Just because I'd checked my e–mail and had gone to borrow a video, I was now crying like a baby. But somehow I couldn't stop. All sorts of things were going through my mind.

What if I made the same mistake in judgement and couldn't fight off the next man? Because I had worried about this ever since the attack in the Caribbean I had called the police station in my village for information on self–defense classes, but the officer I'd spoken with hadn't been able to tell me where to find them. Of my friends, only one had done such a course. It had been a one–off course especially designed for women. The only course that was organized after that was one for senior citizens, men and women, a group that was often victimized on the streets. The people I'd met at sports centers had recommended I take martial arts classes. But the problem with those classes was that it would take quite a while for me to reach the stage where I could defend myself, whereas in a self–defense course I'd learn the techniques straight away.

Even in St. Catherine's, after the rape, I had tried to find a course but never came across one. And in Greece it had been one of the first things I had looked into, but there I'd had no luck either.

However, after having searched the Internet and having looked at the programs of courses that were offered elsewhere, I found out that those self–defense classes not only included practical techniques but also time for discussion and working on assertiveness in everyday life. I knew very well that I needed to work on assertiveness, but I couldn't handle discussing being attacked. Every time I heard the word "rape" part of me died. Clearly, even now, I could not deal with such a confrontation.

I tried some deep breathing to calm myself a bit, but that didn't work. In fact, my breath had become very irregular. It was like the hyperventilating I'd had before, only worse. I really couldn't breathe properly.

And at the same time my mind kept filling up with thoughts. I wasn't fit to lead a normal life! When would the specters of Claudio and the Caribbean criminal leave me? There was no need for them to be there anyway. I knew for sure that I would never forget what I had endured.

I was now gasping for air and was home alone. I had returned from the library around six and hoped that Nicholas would come back straight after work, because Auntie Rosalie and Uncle Stephen had driven to the Catskills for a few days.

I tried very hard to calm myself down, but I couldn't seem to catch my breath anymore.

I now remembered when Irene had told me that my first time had been with Claudio. I had truly hated myself then. She had explained that I had never had sex before. It had been rape, not sex. But that was not how I had felt after the attack. I had felt like a tramp, a slut. I was filthy. And I had just wanted to erase that horrible experience somehow. And now, after all I had been through with Claudio, I wondered if it truly still mattered how many people I slept with and who they were. Sharing that special place with only one person was just not an option anymore.

Realizing once more that I could have had a chance at a first time, after all, was very painful. And all those feelings of despair I'd had before, now came back. Again, it seemed as though every decision I had made since the rape had been wrong and had hurt me even more. I even felt that all this might have happened to me because I had wanted to be victimized. Maybe I had asked for it. I felt I attracted hurt and pain, and there was so much guilt and anger directed at myself, mainly, for not knowing any better. I knew I should have gone to a psychiatrist straight away. And I had gone to one, to a man who hadn't helped me.

I now felt as though I were suffocating. And it frightened me.

But then, suddenly, I heard the door unlocking, and, very soon after that, Nicholas found me in my room and drove me to the clinic, where a nurse used a respiratory device to control my breathing.

After I had begun breathing normally again, the nurse who had soft green eyes and short fair hair, and who I guessed to be about fifty, showed Nicholas and me to a room where a doctor would come to examine me to make sure I was all right.

"It could be a while until the doctor gets here," the nurse said. "More people than usual have been coming in over the past couple of hours. I'm sorry about that."

"That's all right," Nicholas said. "I'm quickly going to rush out and get a sandwich from the store just down the road. I'm pretty hungry. I had an early lunch. She's going to be all right, isn't she?"

"It's almost seven now," the nurse said, glancing at her watch. "You must be starving. Don't worry. She'll be fine."

The nurse then asked me some general questions, inquiring whether I was allergic to any medicine, whether I'd had any major injuries, and then, in the exact same tone of voice, she asked me, "Have you ever been the victim of domestic violence?"

And that started me off again.

I thought back to how Claudio had forced himself on me, how it had taken so long for that vaginal infection to go away, how I had been terribly worried for six months — the second time around — that I might have become infected with HIV, and how, now, I still felt so lonely, so incredibly lonely, not being able to tell anyone the whole truth about everything that had happened with him because I still felt like such a fool. How I longed to be freed of this burden, this trauma that I craved to have erased from my being.

After another episode of gasping for air and shedding tears, the nurse was, once again, able to get me to slow down my breathing.

"It's not just you we ask," she reassured me. "Don't worry. The word "abuse" is not written all over your face."

"Nobody has beaten me if that's what you mean," I sobbed.

"Does your boyfriend hurt you physically or make you do things you don't want to do? Does he not take no for an answer?" she asked me.

"I don't have a boyfriend anymore," I told her. "But, yes, he did do all of those things. But how he hurt me sexually is the most difficult to deal with."

Although I was breathing better now, my tears still streamed down my cheeks as the memories of those nights with Claudio continued to flow back into my mind.

"You know," the nurse continued, "many girls have bad first experiences and are treated with very little respect."

Hearing the nurse speak those words was certainly comforting since I still felt so alone and so ashamed of my horrible sexual experiences.

"I just don't know what to do to stop it from happening again," I sobbed.

The nurse was standing right next to me, and I now noticed her name, Amanda, on her necklace. The letters of her name had been formed by differently colored cubes that hung on a thick brown thread. I thought it looked very pretty.

She must have noticed me looking at her necklace because she said, "The chain it was on broke so now I'm using this. I got it from my ex–boyfriend. I almost married the bastard actually."

I wondered why she still wore it. Claudio had never given me a necklace, but, if he had, I certainly wouldn't wear it. I would probably have given it to charity, just as I had done with the cap from the car rental company.

"Well, why don't I tell you a little story?" Amanda began. "I've talked to girls like you before."

When she spoke like that it was so confrontational. But at the same time I didn't feel like a case alone anymore. No one could ever tell me too many times that I wasn't the only one who had been through an ordeal like I had with Claudio. Holly had never mentioned that her previous boyfriend had hurt her physically. She had just said that she kept going back to him even though she didn't love him because he provided distraction and that not wanting to be touched all the time was a normal reaction for rape victims. Perhaps she had been, just like me, too ashamed to mention that it had been a lot worse than that, although I sincerely hoped that she hadn't suffered as much with him as I had with Claudio.

"I became involved with a man when I was very young," Amanda continued, studying my face carefully. "I know what I'm talking about. I became pregnant the very first time we had sex, and he said he'd marry me. Since I was already pregnant he didn't want to leave it at that one time. I didn't want to sleep with him, but I was so confused that I agreed so that he would definitely marry me. I realized later that I put up with things I shouldn't have, but in those days you couldn't have a baby and not be married. I endured my first sexual experiences, not enjoying them at all, simply because I didn't know any better and because he was only interested in his own pleasure. And he hurt me for it. He made me do things I didn't want to do. I admit, that was a long time ago, but I know it still happens more often than most of us are willing to admit. It's not easy asking for help, is it?"

I shook my head, not being able to find the words. I knew very well how hard it was to tell anyone about the sort of thing Claudio had made me go through, which was why no one knew the entire story. I was way too embarrassed.

"Because you're not sure if there really is something wrong and you're ashamed. Am I right?"

Oh, yes! She was definitely right about that. As a matter of fact, Amanda hit the nail right on the head.

"Maybe you think that's the way it's supposed to be," she went on. "But baby, listen to me and please remember this. A relationship can never really work without the sex being good for both partners. Now I know you can't change the past, but you *can* change the future."

Amanda was living proof that it was indeed possible. All those doubts I'd had about Claudio, I had been right to have them. What an utter fool I had been, convincing myself to believe that it would get better and that he was the one putting up with me. But I was no longer the only fool. And apparently fools really could change, which meant that I could too. And, more importantly, it meant that I might never have to endure the torment that Claudio put me through again. And that was the most relieving thought I think I'd ever had.

"It's not worth spending so much time and going through such agony recovering from what these experiences do to you. If it's not right for you, don't let it happen anymore. You have to think of yourself first and do what's right for you. There are consequences for not taking control soon enough. It works self–destructively. You know that, don't you sweetie?"

And, indeed, I did. This woman could read me like a book. Nobody I had talked to had ever come close to how well she understood me. In the same way Holly had shown understanding of what I had gone through in St. Catherine's,

Amanda now filled the remaining part of the hole inside me by comprehending what I had been through with Claudio. And, finally, I found the solace I had sought from Irene earlier that day.

"I lost the baby," she explained. "That's why I wear the cubes. When I ended the relationship I threw everything away so as to forget, except for the cubes. Look after yourself," she added, taking my hand and squeezing it gently. "Think of yourself first."

"I will," I told her, still trying to take in everything she had just revealed to me. "Thank you for telling me this, Amanda. You don't know how much you've helped me."

"Trust your own instincts," she said, letting go of my hand and leaving the room. "Don't be afraid. All will be well."

A few minutes passed before Nicholas returned. The doctor came about half an hour later and examined me, but I told him I thought it was just a panic attack, and, after having been told to go see my family doctor if I continued experiencing breathing problems, I was released.

Later, in the car, I was overcome with tears of relief. Amanda had made herself vulnerable for my sake. And I was incredibly grateful. She had been there herself. I knew that. And she had managed to make me feel less embarrassed about my sexual ignorance and more importantly, less alone.

"Why are you crying?" Nicholas asked me in a very concerned voice. "Are you all right?"

"I'm all right," I replied, showing him a wide smile through my tears. "Much better than all right actually."

From Nicholas' puzzled expression I concluded that he didn't get it. How could he?

But I did. At long last! Thanks to this selfless act by a complete stranger, for the very first time since that Friday that I was attacked in my apartment, I was genuinely happy.

Chapter 8

About a year later, I went abroad again, to the Caribbean, the islands I had run away from a few years earlier. I knew I'd go back one day, in fifteen to twenty years maybe, to face my fears. I told myself that one day I would go back and walk through the streets of St. Catherine's and be all right. Well, I did.

I won a trip to my Caribbean island. At the travel fair which Auntie Rosalie had urged me to accompany her to in order to show support to a friend of hers who was there to promote trips to Canada, we were all given lottery tickets when we entered the building. And mine turned out to be the lucky draw.

I was reluctant to go. It was ironic that, out of all the places in the world I might have won a trip to, it should be there. In a way it was like going back into the past. It had not been that long ago that I had taken that leap into the unknown in accepting a job abroad. That leap I had taken had burned me badly. I know being raped could have happened anywhere, but it hadn't. It had happened because I had taken a risk I had wanted to take.

My prize was actually just a return ticket for one so I still had to book the accommodation myself. Having worked in the travel industry, I knew that there was always a catch. I thought about it long and hard. And finally I decided that I needed to go, alone.

In all honesty, I really didn't want to go. But then I realized I'd better get it over and done with so that I could get on with my life, once and for all. And that's what I did. I have no regrets. In a way I am proud I dealt with this place so much sooner than expected and so much more successfully.

I had chosen a hotel in another town and, on the day after my arrival, I took the bus to St. Catherine's where the statue of the saint who gave the town its name still stood there watching over the square, the saint who had been unable to protect me. Standing about two yards away from her I looked up to see her face. She knew. I sat down on the ledge at her feet. The stone was warm and somehow comforting.

The police station was directly opposite where I sat. I had often thought of going back to press charges. But now, after about three and a half years, the term of limitation had been reached. Auntie Rosalie had always discouraged me to go back or to try to press charges from home, and, when I had brought it up, Irene had never encouraged me. I thought back to a discussion I'd had with Auntie Rosalie.

"It's all very well saying you need to do this if you want to see him pay," she had said one evening in the kitchen, "but if you press charges and there is a court case, don't fool yourself into believing he will definitely be punished. You've just gone through hell. Imagine what it would be like, facing him again, explaining what happened to a judge and jury, repeating your story over and over again."

"But it's the only way to make him pay," I had said, confused and desperate.

"I know," she told me. "But in the best case, all he will get is some time in prison. Do you want to be around when he gets out? Maybe his friends will take revenge. Also, take into account the fact that the defense lawyers are going to go out of their way to make you look like a tramp. They'll say whatever they want to about the way you were dressed and your behavior. You already feel guilty, which is to their advantage. Couldn't you have done more to fight him off? Are you sure you made it clear to him that you didn't want it? Are you really that strong? The bottom line is that he wins no matter what. You have suffered terribly. The question is, how much more are you willing to suffer because of him?"

By then I had begun crying bitterly. Auntie Rosalie had taken my hand and continued. "Don't fool yourself into believing that you can combine a court case like that with your studies or a career. Especially if you don't win. Then what? If you lose, you'll end up having to deal with the fact that society approves of what he did to you. He will be a free man. And do you honestly think he will let you off the hook for causing him public humiliation? You'll always be looking over your shoulder. If the police didn't help you when you went to them, there must have been a reason. Maybe they were trying to protect him. Stay away from there. You've already been hurt enough."

All of that did make sense. But how could criminals like him be stopped then? Having encountered that monster after the rape was indescribably horrifying. And even now I continually worried about seeing him, on the street, on the bus, anywhere. I knew I'd always be looking over my shoulder anyway.

When I reported the crime to the police they gave me the number of the rapist's file, and I kept it for a long time, but, much later, I threw it away because I believed that by holding on to it I was not letting go of what had happened. I felt it somehow prevented me from moving on.

My main concern will always be that he might go on raping unsuspecting young women, women who, like me, let him into their house, although I doubt that I was the first person he raped. But Auntie Rosalie tried to reassure me.

"He probably bettered himself and is leading a good life now," she had said.

I had been extremely angry with her for saying that, but I realized later that she had said it to comfort me, to try to convince me to let it go. She must have realized that it was much more important that I got on with my life and put the entire ordeal behind me than that I kept on beating myself up over leaving him unpunished. Auntie Rosalie said he might have bettered his life. I suppose that was her attempt at making my guilt level drop. If he truly had changed, no other girl would be at risk of experiencing my trauma. But I will never believe it.

And now, although I had failed to put him behind bars, I had returned to the Caribbean to face my fears. This trip actually represented a true personal challenge. I was proud of myself. And that was a wonderful feeling.

Auntie Rosalie and Nicholas couldn't understand why I would want to go back there and were worried about me. They asked me several times if this was truly what I wanted to do. But Charlene told me to see it as a sign.

"It's a sign you shouldn't ignore," she said. "It's your destiny. Fate is telling you to banish what happened to you in St. Catherine's from your life for good."

Although I realized very well that I would never be able to erase the experience from my memory, I knew what she meant. I had to learn to take chances again. Because great opportunities don't come by often in life. You have to reach out and grab them before they pass you by. And this was one of them I meant to have.

Epilogue

Although sex seems to be such an important part of life for many people, it is still something I somehow try to avoid. In fact, it is the first thing I worry about when I consider starting a new relationship. I even catch myself looking at men on the street or on the bus, wondering if they would be caring partners in bed. I don't think of sexual fantasies but merely ask myself, "Would he be gentle and understanding? Would he put my needs before his own?"

The frightening part of it all is that I am afraid of trusting the wrong person again. It will always be a risk. But will I ever have enough courage to take that risk?

I tell myself I don't miss anything. Why complicate my life? Maybe I don't feel as though I am missing out by not having sexual intercourse because I have never had a positive experience with it.

Then again, I still want to experience the real thing. I know that it is an illusion to think that I will ever be able to compensate for what has happened to me sexually for good. But I don't want to miss out on all the other aspects of a romantic relationship: the laughing, the caring, the love, the commitment, the sense of completeness, the knowledge of being special, the feeling of being important. But perhaps now I do want to save myself for that special person.

Some people tell me that if I'm not open to these sorts of relationships, men will sense it and not approach me. Even when I am approached I don't take much interest. Maybe when the right person comes along I will. Maybe not.

***

I find it incredibly difficult to accept the ordeal. I feel that so many incidents still remind me of the rape. Sometimes, I still see fragments of what happened to me and I am never truly alone. The trauma has become a part of me. It will never go away completely. It is now part of who I am. I know that I should try to cherish that part of me because it has made me stronger. The scar on my body and soul that will never disappear. Maybe I should be proud of it, proud of what I have endured. I have matured because of it, and I have learned a lot.

I have learned not to judge people so quickly. Other people have been through ordeals of their own. Everyone has their story. And believe me, you cannot tell just by looking at someone. That is one of the reasons why I find people so fascinating. People you don't understand, those you seem to have figured out so easily, and those you'd never suspect of having endured anything — they all could be carrying the most incredible experiences with them, although you might never know about them. I love people more now than before.

And I enjoy the mysteries of life. I don't even want to know the scientific explanation of certain phenomena. I like experiencing things without necessarily knowing how they are possible or how they exist. I still don't like surprises, but I do enjoy rainbows and eclipses, coincidences that aren't really coincidental. I will never understand everything there is to understand, and I no longer want to.

This does not mean I am no longer eager to learn, because I am. I definitely want to learn more languages to be able to talk to people I wouldn't be able to converse with otherwise. Being curious, reading, listening, discovering new things — all of this makes me hungry for more. There is very little I am not interested in. The world is such an interesting place. It would be a shame not to make the most of your time here.

Sometimes other things take priority: an illness you need to recover from, a loss you have to mourn, or any other trauma or situation you have to deal with first. Irene said I had to mourn first before I could carry on. How long it takes is different for each individual she said. She encouraged me and told me I was the only one who would know what felt right for me.

I don't want to sleep with a man merely to try to have a positive sexual experience. I wouldn't have done that before, and I won't do it now. I like to think I have some principles and self–respect left yet. I want to start afresh with my standards and norms intact. I don't want to live a promiscuous life, trying to experience as many exhilarating sexual encounters as possible.

In fact, I just want to be me. I'd say a part of me is lost, although maybe it was merely transformed. I have evolved and will continue to evolve throughout my life. In many ways I am not who I was before, but I feel I can still like who I am. As I am the one who will always have to live with myself, it is important that I approve of who I am.

For a long time I was not ambitious. I didn't care much about a career. I did obtain a business degree, but I do not have the ambition to fill an important position at a prestigious firm which is what I wanted when I was little. I wanted to be someone I could be proud of, and I still feel that way, but I am more at peace with myself.

I try not to demand things of myself or rush myself to accomplish things quickly. Instead, I try to live each day at a time, allowing myself to relax and take my time. I always wanted everything immediately. And although I am still not a patient person, I am trying to give myself a break.

I might not have accepted the rape completely, but I still want to live and enjoy life.

I do wonder where I'd be now if that monster hadn't interfered with my life, although I realize that I will never know. Fate decided I should take this turn on my journey. Perhaps the road I am on now and the one I was on before will come together again after a while. Perhaps they won't. But I try not to give that too much thought. I am on my way again. I have stumbled and fallen. But I have picked myself up again. There are bruises that hurt. But the pain slowly diminishes until it's bearable. I am walking on with my head held high. Although my legs still tremble, I am walking. Not so long from now I'll walk more confidently. I'll be able to go faster if I want to, to take risks. But for the moment, I try to walk steadily, prudently so as not to trip.

Acknowledgements

On various occasions, my psychiatrist had told me that I should write down everything I was feeling, but I could not. The confrontation with those deep–rooted emotions was too great for me to handle then.

One morning, a few months after I had stopped seeing her, I got up and began to write. I wrote about my pain, my loathing, my rage, my despair, my frustration and the ever–hovering hope that things would get better.

After about a year of pouring my heart out on the pages that were now filled with resentment, jealousy, hatred, disgust and so much anger, I came to the stage where I had said everything I wanted to say, at least once. A close friend in whom I confided asked me if I would delete everything, sort of like deleting the whole experience from my life. But I needed and wanted more satisfaction than that. I should, I thought, at least be allowed to print the pages and then rip them up, reducing them in the way in which the experiences had reduced me.

Instead, I decided to place my writing on a shelf at the back of my closet in case one day I might meet someone, someone who could find some kind of solace in reading my revealed emotions and feel less alone, less of a fool.

But I couldn't move on. I had nothing to live for. Nothing mattered enough for me to focus on the future and leave the past behind. So I figured I had two choices. I could go on hating the world until it would drive me to actually commit suicide, or I could attempt to do something positive for someone else until I was finally able to do something positive for myself. I opted for the latter.

I began again and attempted to write a story that would capture how I had felt and what I had thought while struggling through these traumatic experiences. The sole purpose of this piece of writing is that it will hopefully help another. If it makes only one person feel less alone, less guilty, less filthy, or encourages just one individual to get out of an abusive relationship, then I feel that I have accomplished what I set out to do.

***

I am grateful to all the loving supportive individuals I am fortunate to have in my life. You know who you are.

I thank those of you who have been there since the early stages and those who joined later. The colors of your ever–growing bouquet of love are bright, warm and plentiful; the aromas sweet and uplifting; and your touch gentle, tender and encouraging. I feel blessed to have each and every one of you in my life, and I love you all.

Printed in the United Kingdom
by Lightning Source UK Ltd.
107258UKS00001B/26